PUFFIN BOOKS

Editor: Kaye Webb

THE CHILDREN OF THE HOUSE

'Laura Hatton,' said Laura, glaring at her face in the mirror, 'what could be worse than being Laura Hatton?' Suddenly everything was too much for her. At least her brothers, Tom, the heir to the family estate, and Hugh, were able to go away to school and leave the strictness and grim economy of home, but she had to stay there for years longer, wearing childish dresses, knowing nothing of the world until she was married off.

It's true they were Hattons of Stanford Hall, living in one of the grandest houses in England, but no one outside would ever have guessed what it meant to be one of the children, the economies that were made in their schooling, their clothes, and even their food, the lack of love or interest from their parents, and how they had learned to play in silence and never to pass in front of their father's study window in case he saw them. The truth was that their mother was too devoted to her house to worry much about whether they were happy, and their father never thought twice about them except to exhort them to gratitude.

And so Tom, Laura, Hugh and Margaret were happiest when they were together and their parents were away, and turned for affection to the butler, the groom, the gardener and the maids, until the First World War came along and ended their story.

In many ways this is a sad book, with its tale of a rift between children and parents and so many missed opportunities for happiness, but it should appeal to anyone who likes a grown-up story and who likes to follow the fortunes of one family over a number of years.

For readers of twelve and over, particularly girls.

Cover design by Shirley Hughes

The Children of the House

*

BRIAN FAIRFAX-LUCY
and
PHILIPPA PEARCE

*

Illustrated by
JOHN SERGEANT

PUFFIN BOOKS

Puffin Books, Penguin Books Ltd, Harmondsworth, Middlesex, England
Penguin Books, 625 Madison Avenue, New York, New York 10022, U.S.A.
Penguin Books Australia Ltd, Ringwood, Victoria, Australia
Penguin Books Canada Ltd, 41 Steelcase Road West, Markham, Ontario, Canada
Penguin Books (N.Z.) Ltd, 182–190 Wairau Road, Auckland 10, New Zealand

—

First published by Longmans Young Books 1968
Published in Puffin Books 1970
Reprinted 1972, 1976

—

Copyright © Brian Fairfax-Lucy and Philippa Pearce, 1968

—

Made and printed in Great Britain by
Cox & Wyman Ltd,
London, Reading and Fakenham
Set in Linotype Pilgrim

AUTHOR'S NOTE

I would like to express my deep indebtedness to Philippa Pearce, who has adapted *The Children of the House* from a story which I originally intended for adults, and made it one that can be enjoyed and understood by children.

The Children of the House was written from a memory of a way of life now vanished; but the people and places named here have no actuality except in the imagination of the author – and of the reader.

B.F-L.

PROLOGUE

No children live at Stanford Hall now.

No one lives there except the old caretaker and his wife. Every weekday in summer the caretaker throws open the great gates to coachloads of sightseers that come down the long avenue to the Hall. They are shown round the state rooms: the drawing-room with cushions plumped upon chairs and sofas, with the gilt harp standing ready and the spinet open, as if for some musical evening that never begins; the dining-room with its long table covered to the floor with double damask, with branched candelabra down the middle, and twenty places laid with silver, glass and china – but nobody ever eats and drinks here; the library with a thousand calf-bound volumes that nobody ever opens.

The sightseers are not shown the rest of the house – the smaller rooms where the master and mistress lived, and where their children came to them; the servants' quarters behind the baize door; the children's own rooms – nursery and schoolroom and the rest. The children's things are still here – the rocking-horse, the collection of birds' eggs; but the children are gone.

No children have lived here since before the First World War, over fifty years ago – since the time of Laura, Thomas, Hugh and Margaret Hatton. This is their story.

I

BEFORE going to sleep last night Hugh had beaten his head
repeatedly on the pillow: one – two – three – four – five. He
must be awake at five o'clock. And now he was awake – or
at least half-awake; and he could not for the life of him
remember the reason for urgency.

From over the edge of the bedclothes, the nursery looked
just as usual. The rocking-horse reminded him that this
morning he must ride round the farms with Papa. It would
be dull, and miserable too: what might Papa say? what
might the horse do? – and then – oh *then* what might Papa
say?

Beyond the head of the rocking-horse he saw familiar pic-
tures on the nursery wall: the white cat and the green parrot
staring at each other; the anxious-looking little girl called
'Wait for Me', who always reminded him of Victor's sister,
Evie; the drawing of W. G. Grace. He liked the drawing best
because he loved cricket; but what a pity about the black
beard! The beard made his hero look like Grandpapa, whose
portrait hung in the great hall, a Hatton among the generations and centuries of Stanfords. Grandpapa Hatton had
died when Hugh was a very little boy, but Papa still quoted
him as a great and godly industrialist. His motto had been,
'Look after the pennies and the pounds will look after themselves.' Hugh thought he must have been a mean man. A
careful man. An unadventurous man –

Adventure! Suddenly Hugh remembered why he had to
wake early. He jumped out of bed at once, afraid that he
might be too late; then reassured himself. From the sun and
the silence, it could not be much after five. Nevertheless,
time must not be wasted. For this was the very first day of
the holidays for them all; this very evening Tom came home.

He dressed quickly, opened the nursery door with caution and tiptoed along the passage into the room where the other two slept. He threw himself on top of his elder sister's bed: 'Get up, Laura!'

Sleepily Laura began to rouse herself, tossing her long hair from her face. In the other bed Margaret burrowed deeper into sleep.

'Hurry, both of you.' He was by the window now, looking out. 'There's mist rising from the river; it's going to be hot. And last night in bed I planned our adventure for the first day of the holidays – something to tell Tom about.'

'What?' Margaret asked. Laura had set about waking her and had done it thoroughly, as she did most things.

'We take the punt and go downstream to find eggs.'

Margaret could not swim, so she said, 'We'll get into awful trouble if anyone drowns; and we'll get into it anyway if we're caught.'

'We shan't be caught, if we hurry now,' Laura said. 'And Hugh's right: we must have something to tell Tom.'

Laura was already flinging on her clothes and Margaret had to do the same. Without brushing their hair or washing, all three crept along the passage and down the back stairs to the back door.

They paused in the stone-flagged passage, listening intently; but the baize door, solid and almost sound-proof, separated this wing of the house from the front, where their parents slept. With the baize door shut and no servants yet about, it was most unlikely that they could be heard by anyone. The only possible exception was Walter Mark, the butler, who slept downstairs on this side of the baize door, and Walter was Hugh's best friend.

As usual, they found the back door double-locked and bolted, with a heavy iron bar right across. Slotted into this bar was a thin, easily-vibrating strip of metal which held a small bell aloft. Similar bells were set every night on the bars of all the doors and ground floor windows. These were the burglar-alarms of Stanford Hall.

Laura, as the tallest, had the job of removing the bell from the back door. It gave the faintest tinkle, and she suppressed a laugh: 'I hope we aren't disturbing Walter.'

Hugh was drawing the bolts, while Margaret struggled with the big key in its lock. He said: 'Walter told me he would never wake, anyway, if a burglar came this way.' Walter Mark slept next door to the room where the family silver was kept, to guard it.

Margaret paused to say, 'But I don't think any burglar *could* get in through this door, do you?'

They knew that she was trying to reassure herself, because she had always been frightened of burglars and ghosts and all the rest. Laura, who had never been frightened of any of them, teased her: 'But some burglars are so clever, aren't they, Hugh? And stealthy and silent as cats.'

'Shut up, Laura. And, Meg, get on with the unlocking. Use both hands to the key.'

The key turned at last; the door swung open; and one after the other they slipped out, past Jet, the black retriever, in his kennel – out into a world empty and all their own. In the yard the stable clock showed not quite five o'clock, and their spirits rose. They had an hour before the grooms and household servants started their day's work, and over two whole hours before their father and mother were called.

They ran across the gravel, on to the dew-wet grass, and so round the house to the river. The Hall stood in wide parklands, through which the River Teal wound its way, passing close behind the house. Here the children could not be seen or heard by anyone who mattered. Their parents' bedroom looked out on to the court at the front of the house. That circumstance, indeed, had decided Hugh upon this particular expedition.

The punt was already in the water by the landing-stage, chained but not padlocked. The children clambered in,

Laura bringing the chain aboard at Hugh's order, Hugh himself taking the pole. He began to punt, while the two girls leant over the sides to trail their fingers in the dark water. They had not forgotten nest-hunting, but the reeds along these banks were never hopeful.

Slowly the punt rounded a bend in the river and a clear stretch of water came into sight before woods ran down to the banks. Willows and tall bushes grew here, and the river narrowed. This was the place. Hugh punted alongside an island of yellow waterlilies and weeds.

Laura was standing up now. 'There's a duck's nest, I think. Built on old pieces of wood. Careful, Hugh.'

Hugh ran the punt to within a foot of where Laura was pointing. Margaret was nearest: she reached out, took one of the large, greenish-white eggs, and handed it to Laura. Laura shook it gently: 'Addled.'

'Ducks' eggs are really over,' Hugh said. 'Better a moorhen's nest, if we could find one.' He released the pole from the position in which he had been keeping it to steady the punt, and drove them on. The sun had now risen high enough to come sifting through the foliage, blotching and dappling all it fell upon. A slight breeze moved the leaves, making the blotches and dapples dance in a bewildering way before the eyes.

Margaret gave an 'Oooh!' of fear.

'What is it now?'

'There's someone watching from among the trees.'

'Dan,' said Laura. Dan Power was the Stanford gamekeeper.

'Not Dan. Someone who – who doesn't want us to see him.'

But, as if in contradiction of this last remark, a boy stepped out from among the trees on the bank, raising his hand in greeting. He was Hugh's age, or younger. They all recognized him.

'Victor!' said Hugh, pleased. The girls only stared in

silence, until Laura said, 'Aren't you afraid of Dan Power catching you?'

'No. He doesn't mean to, but he gives good warning of his coming. Besides, I'm not poaching.'

'What are you doing?' Margaret asked – a question the others might have liked to put, but they were afraid of seeming inquisitive. Victor ignored the question, and addressed himself to Hugh: 'You never came the other day.'

Hugh was embarrassed. 'It was our governess. She kept us indoors in the schoolroom, learning German verbs.' Victor said nothing to this: to Hugh his silence seemed critical, even scornful. 'I shan't be having lessons from a governess much longer. I'm being sent away to a proper school. And the governess has gone now, anyway – gone back to Germany for her holidays.'

'How about your coming tomorrow, then?'

Hugh said eagerly, 'Oh, yes!' and then, remembering, 'well, I don't know. Tom will be home.'

'Tom likes to lead expeditions of us,' said Laura. 'We're on one now to get into practice.'

'Hugh is leading this expedition instead of Tom, as Tom isn't back,' said Margaret.

'For moorhens' eggs,' said the substitute for a leader.

Victor looked as if he had little opinion of all this; but he only said to Hugh: 'I thought you had a moorhen's egg in the collection.'

'These are for eating.'

'Well, you've just passed two nests'; and Victor pointed to a spot behind them. Laura clicked her tongue in annoyance, and Hugh began to manoeuvre the punt backwards, closer to the bank. Here trees leant out over the water, so that the base of their trunks almost breasted it. Rafts of flotsam and islands of mud and stone had been left by the course of the current. Not a good stretch for navigation, except by water-fowl. On the far side of a mudbank were two moorhens' nests. Hugh brought the punt close enough for the girls to lean over and – with some difficulty – reach them.

'Ten in this one,' said Laura. 'And warm.' She was handling them gently. 'But not fresh, I think: they seem too heavy.'

'The other clutch is probably fresher,' Victor said from the bank.

'Six here,' Margaret said. 'What shall I do?'

'Take three out of the six,' Hugh said. Then, 'What's the matter, Victor?'

Victor had moved as if in alarm. 'That gamekeeper's coming.'

'Dan's a friend of ours.'

'Not particularly of mine.' Victor began moving along the bank away from them, clearly on the point of withdrawing altogether.

Hugh was desperate not to lose him. 'Here! Wait a minute!' He dug his pole in hard and pushed strongly on it, but in his anxiety he misjudged several things. The punt shot forward, as he had meant, but the pole had been driven deeply into a mud bank and remained there when he tried to withdraw it. The punt and the pole were parting company, and in a matter of seconds Hugh had to choose between them.

'Leave the pole!' Victor whispered urgently from his distance.

'The pole!' said Laura.

'Oh! Oh! Oh!' said Margaret.

In the middle of whichever thing he was doing – and Hugh was not at all clear anyway – he changed his mind. Both punt and pole went from him, and he landed with a splash, knee-deep in mud and water.

Meanwhile, Victor had disappeared, and there was Dan.

Dan Power, the indirect cause of their disaster, was now their saviour. He secured the drifting punt by means of the chain, which Laura threw to him. He then boarded it at a point from which he was able to secure the pole. Finally he secured Hugh, who had obediently stayed exactly where he was, lest otherwise he should lose his boots in the mud of the river-bed.

Even with his boots, Hugh's appearance appalled the imagination of the others in the punt. 'I don't like to think what Sir Robert or her Ladyship would say,' said Dan.

'Oooh!' said Margaret.

'Can we get him clean before anyone sees him?' said Laura.

Dan thought it could be done. He would punt them home at once; and, while he did so, Hugh must strip off boots and stockings. Dan would wash them under the stable-pump, while Hugh and the other two slipped into the house – with luck, unnoticed.

In this reasonable hope, they relaxed. Laura stealthily felt for the three eggs hidden under a fold of her skirt, and said, 'Did you really think we were poachers, Dan?' She was gratified at the idea.

Dan said briefly, between pushes on the pole, that he had heard voices and had come to see. At this time of year he was always about early in the woods, because of the young pheasants. He also had to see to the rabbit traps. 'And' – sourly – 'someone had been letting rabbits out o' the traps this morning.'

Margaret had a bright idea. 'Perhaps *that* was what Victor was –'

Laura's foot fell heavily upon Margaret's toe, so that her sentence ended in a little shriek of pain and was never otherwise finished; Hugh looked shaken.

Dan glanced from one to the other doubtfully. His eyes narrowed; but all he said was: 'I don't know what Sir Robert would say, Master Hugh, if he knew you went bird's-nesting with that schoolmaster's son from the village, as you do.'

'Victor knows really a lot about birds,' Hugh said. 'He got

a jackdaw's egg each for our collections; he knew where to go. He says one day he'll get a heron's egg.'

Dan laughed shortly. 'Not he!' The herons of the Teal built their ramshackle nests in colonies in the tops of tall trees with few low branches. The herons knew their business.

The punt was now up to the landing-stage, and Dan Power's plan was carried out. As the children came round the house to the back door they met William Kemble, the head groom, leading a file of horses, nine in all, out of the stable yard. But William Kemble was their friend.

As they went in through the back door, they were met by Walter Mark, full of anxiety. 'I knew you were out.' Then, seeing Hugh, 'Whatever have you been up to? No boots, no stockings!'

'Dan's washing them and bringing them.'

'Go on up quickly and get tidy. I'll see Dan, and send up a pair of clean boots. Hurry. Hurry.'

They never met their parents until after breakfast, which was now brought to them by Elsie, the little between-maid. She was on their side. They would never forget that, when she had been very new in service at the Hall, she had carried a plum-cake up to them from the dining-room, under the impression that the children had the same food as their parents.

The gong sounded for prayers. Soberly the children went down the front stairs to the dining-room. They entered in order of age, Laura first, and in the same order kissed their parents and took their places. Walter Mark and Ernest, the footman, brought in two benches for the servants to sit on, and Walter handed Sir Robert his Bible and Prayer-book. No one ever spoke, and there was a particular silence as the rest of the household staff filed in – Lady Hatton's French maid, Hortense; Mrs Ashley, the cook; Alice, the head housemaid; Elsie, the between-maid; the under-housemaid; and the kitchen-maid. Ernest shut the door after the last of them, and then he and Walter took their seats at the ends of the two rows.

Sir Robert read from the Bible. Then, at his 'Let us pray', everyone turned to kneel. This was the moment when Hugh and Margaret – Laura felt herself growing too old for it – sometimes tried to catch the eye of a friend from beyond the baize door, to force even a quarter-smile; but today neither was in the mood. They all sensed trouble brewing.

The servants had filed out again in the order of their entry; Ernest and Walter had removed the benches, and themselves.

'Shut the door, Laura,' said their father. 'I wish to speak to you all.'

Their hearts sank. Could their adventure already be known; or was this just an ordinary lecture?

'Now,' said Sir Robert, when Laura was back in her place. 'The holidays have started and tonight Tom comes home. I warn you that I will not tolerate any wildness, lateness for meals, untidiness, disobedience, or misbehaviour in any way. I know that Tom is often your ringleader, and if he does not mend his ways, I shall send him away with a tutor. I am also prepared, if necessary, to hire a tutor here so that you do lessons all through the holidays. Do you understand?'

'Yes, Papa.'

Lady Hatton spoke more gently. 'But, of course, we know you will all wish to start your holidays by being good.' They realized that they ought to feel guilty: it was so much too late to start the holidays by being good, since this morning.

'Hugh,' said his father, 'you will ride this morning.'

'Yes, Papa.'

'But as I shall be busy with papers, you will ride with William.' The clouds rolled back from Hugh's morning: ride with *William*!

Their mother took over now. 'This afternoon Papa and I

have to attend a meeting. I want you all to take a rice-pudding to old Mrs Higgs in the village. You can go in the pony-trap – Laura had better drive. After that, you may play in the garden.'

'Be careful not to spoil your clothes in any way,' said their father, 'as I certainly cannot afford to get you new ones.'

'Now all of you run along to the schoolroom and read your books. Be especially quiet, as Papa has several people to see in his study.'

'No running up and down the passage,' said Sir Robert.

'No, indeed,' said their mother.

They were dismissed; they were safe. Their adventure was undiscovered, after all. And this afternoon, after the expedition in the pony-trap, they could boil the moorhen's eggs. In fact, since their parents would be out, the whole afternoon was theirs. And in the evening Tom would come home.

2

OLD Mrs Higgs said she was very thankful for the rice-pudding for Mr Higgs, who was upstairs in bed with a mustard plaster on him. It would do him good just to know that a pudding had come for him from the big house.

She made the children come into the little cottage and sit in a row on the horsehair sofa, while she talked. She exclaimed at how much they were all growing. She remembered their being born. She remembered all that excitement before Miss Laura was born, because she was the first baby. And the same excitement before Master Tom, and great celebrations afterwards, because he was a boy. For that matter she remembered their mother as a little girl, Miss Linda Stanford. So pretty; and the only child: the heiress. And she remembered as if it were yesterday – but it must be a good fifteen years ago – her marrying Sir Robert. That would be – let's see – in 1892. And then the first baby – that was Miss Laura, of course . . .

Gently but without stop Mrs Higgs talked her way to and fro among the generations. The children felt their precious afternoon slipping from them.

But now Mrs Higgs was moving into the more recent past. She was taking down from the mantelpiece three smooth stones which looked like kidney beans: she said that they were gall stones taken out of Mr Higgs last year, and she was ever so proud of them. She handed them round.

'It must have been painful,' said Laura, as the eldest, not knowing what else to say. 'And now I'm afraid we must – '

'That it was,' Mrs Higgs agreed heartily. 'But he's thankful to be spared, and to have his job.' Mr Higgs, like nearly everybody else in the village, worked on the Stanford estate.

Margaret had been fidgeting more and more on the sofa: stiff horse-hairs were sticking out of it and into the plump flesh of her legs. Laura, observing her desperately, managed to get out that they really must be going. The pony would not stand for long with the flies about.

The children had a few more visits to make in the village for their mother. They were homeward bound when Margaret suddenly stood up in the pony-trap. 'Look, there's Victor's sister!' She began to call her: 'Evie!'

'For goodness' sake!' Laura said, and Hugh pulled her down quite roughly.

'But we could have talked to Evie!' Margaret protested. Here had been a chance, for Evie was not usually about out of doors: she had poor health and spent much of her time in bed. 'We could have told her the end of the adventure this morning, and then she could have told Victor.'

'I daresay,' said Laura. 'And then half the village would see how well we know them, and sooner or later Papa and Mama would get to hear of it!'

Margaret sank back, and they drove on homewards.

At home, their parents had already gone out, so the three children gathered freely in the butler's pantry with Walter Mark: he and Hugh discussed the cricket news; Margaret nursed the stable cat, never otherwise allowed into the house; and Laura daydreamed – daydreamed of being Tom. Then they played Wolf outside until tea-time. Schoolroom tea was as meagre as usual, with no cake; but afterwards they took the three moorhen's eggs from their hiding-place and boiled them over a fire in a trench dug in the seclusion of one of the shrubberies.

Hugh worried that their parents might come back in the middle of all this, and Laura suggested that they should provide themselves with watering-cans full of water: 'If

necessary, we could put the fire out at once and pretend we were just watering the flowers for Mama.'

'Genius!' Hugh said handsomely. Laura, as a girl, was his subordinate, but a useful one.

There was no emergency, however. After they had eaten the eggs, they had time to put their makeshift saucepan back in the toolshed, destroy all obvious traces of the fire, and clean their smoky faces and hands in the soft water from the butt. All this before they heard the carriage swing through the arch to the front door.

As their parents went into the house to change, the children of the house could be seen watering the flower-borders with their cans.

'What a wonderful day!' said Margaret, casting her spray in happy spirals.

At the usual time that evening they went to the drawing-room to say good night to their mother. She spoke of Tom's coming: 'Papa wants you all to be in bed when he arrives. As a special treat he is having dinner with us. He goes straight to bed afterwards in the nursery with you, Hugh – but you will be asleep, of course. Papa thinks it best that none of you see Tom until the morning. Papa knows that otherwise you would become over-excited. Be careful not to make a noise as you go to bed, as Papa has had a busy day. Now you can all kneel down and say your prayers.'

They had said their prayers and kissed their mother and were leaving, when she called them back: 'If Papa is in his study, you may say good night to him.' To their relief he was not.

They had eaten their supper of bread and milk and were ready for bed. The gong summoned their parents to dinner. For an hour after this, and often for longer, they could play and talk in peace, without any fear of being caught in each other's rooms.

'His train must be late,' observed Laura. 'They're not waiting dinner for him.'

Hugh said, 'When Tom does arrive and goes into the dining-room, we can nip down the back stairs and hear from Walter how he is.'

'We might get something off the dishes as they go back to the kitchen,' said Margaret. 'They've my favourite tonight: fried potatoes. I could smell them.'

'Oh!' they sighed. 'Oh, if only Tom would arrive soon.'

Soon they heard it – the first faint rattle of the dog-cart from up the drive. They hung over the bars of the nursery window, looking down into the stable yard. They waved as the dog-cart drove up to the back door, but they did not call out, for fear of being overheard by the wrong person.

There was Tom. Ernest came out of the house and took his trunk from the back of the cart. Then Ernest and Tom disappeared from view indoors.

'Someone's coming,' Hugh said. 'Back to your room –

quick!' The girls disappeared, and a moment afterwards he heard Tom's voice at the foot of the stairs, and then the foreign voice of Hortense, the French maid: 'No, no, for Sir Robert is expecting you. Go quickly to dinner.'

'But surely I can see them first?'

'No, they are asleep in bed. Go.' Hugh laughed to himself.

The children waited. They timed their next move perfectly: they were along the passage together and down the back stairs in a flash, just as Ernest was starting out with Tom's dinner. He nearly dropped it as they burst upon him.

'Hi!' said Hugh. 'Let's have some fried potatoes.'

'Oh, not too many. Otherwise her Ladyship will notice: she knows how many went out of the dining-room to keep warm.'

Hugh took for them all, but moderately. 'That's enough now,' said Ernest uneasily. He went on as the dining-room bell rang.

They divided the potatoes. 'Now to waylay Walter for the news,' said Laura.

They had not long to wait. Walter came, stopped, and said, as if announcing a distinguished guest: 'Her Ladyship wishes me to inform you that you have stolen her goods, and Sir Robert is much distressed and is on his way.'

They stared at him, frozen. Then they saw the smile that came over his face and Laura seized his hand: 'Don't frighten us so. Tell us what they're talking about.'

'Well, Master Tom looks well, and Sir Robert's been asking him how he's done at cricket and at his work.'

'Yes?' Hugh said anxiously.

'I gathered that he'd done well at both. Then the usual about money, and talk about Master Tom's being extravagant. Apparently he didn't ought to have taken a cab across London; and her Ladyship says how could he have got his trunk across if he hadn't. Oh yes, and her Ladyship thinks

there should perhaps be a little party for you all some time, but Sir Robert says all that sort of thing is a waste of money. People only come to that sort of thing for what they can get out of you. His father always told him there were too many ways of wasting money, and it was true.'

At that moment the bell rang again and Walter had to go. The children vanished upstairs.

Later, when Tom came to bed, they were awake and waiting for him. Laura and Margaret came promptly from their bedroom to the nursery. Hugh was sitting up in bed; and Tom straddled the rocking-horse, like a general mounted and in command of his army.

'Mama said you'd started the holidays well by being good; and Papa said I was not to begin leading you into any mischief, or we should all be punished.'

'We haven't really been good at all,' Margaret said eagerly.

'We went down the river for moorhens' eggs,' said Laura.

'We saw Victor; and I fell in,' said Hugh.

'What adventure were you thinking of for tomorrow morning, Tom?' asked Laura.

But Tom did not like being pushed into things – even into leadership. He yawned languidly. 'A fellow needs rest sometimes. Not tomorrow. Later.'

They were disappointed, but accepted his command. After all, this was no surrender, no retreat; more like a bivouac that the general had ordered.

Tom yawned again – a great gaping yawn that was forced out of him willy-nilly. 'A fellow must go to bed some time,' he said.

The clock on the stable block showed ten. The children of the house were in bed at last. The servants were going to bed. The only people still up were Lady Hatton alone in the library, Sir Robert alone in his study, and Walter Mark, now tapping on the study door for his last orders.

Sir Robert was deep among estate accounts and other papers. 'I wish not to be interrupted. No one need stay up to see to the lamps and the fires; I myself will be responsible.'

'Very good, Sir Robert.'

Walter withdrew to the other side of the baize door. In his private opinion, something was up tonight. He made ready to retire to his little bedroom next door to the pantry. Before he did so, he opened the baize door a crack. Through it he could see the study door, and it was open, and the room empty. Sir Robert had gone to the library, where her ladyship was reading. That meant trouble, and Walter thought he knew what kind of trouble, too. He let the baize door swing to, cutting his world off from theirs, thankfully. Then he undressed to his underclothes, got into bed, and blew out his candle.

As usual, Walter Mark was right. In the library Sir Robert was talking to his wife about the problems of the Stanford estate. Lady Hatton listened, at first looking into the fire; and in spite of the fire, she shivered. At the time of their marriage, the great estate she had inherited had been almost bankrupt. She knew that only her husband's money and his hard business head had saved it. She knew that, ever since, he had made it pay its way – just. She also knew that he hated the place.

'The agent tells me,' Sir Robert was saying, 'that we face the prospect of having two of our farms unlet. This is very serious. He advises selling.'

'I won't consider selling any of Tom's inheritance.'

Tom was the heir: that was his importance. At Laura's birth, her mother had cried bitterly because she was a girl; and when Tom was born, she had said they must have another boy, in case he died. So Hugh was born. And then Margaret, for no particular reason at all.

Sir Robert was saying doggedly: 'The agent suggests that we sell Lower Barn Farm. It is an outlying one.'

Lady Hatton looked up from the fire at that. 'The impertinence of that common little man! Lower Barn was the farm my father liked best. He kept his race-horses there.'

'You have never understood, Linda, that times change and that we cannot afford – literally *cannot* afford – not to change with them. That farm must be sold.'

'He kept his race-horses there. The gallops are still there. One day Tom or Hugh will be able to train their horses there just as my father did.'

'Neither Tom nor Hugh is interested in horses – Hugh is afraid of a horse. Laura is the only one, and she's a girl. Anyway, the farm must be sold.'

'No.'

'The farm must be sold. This small part of the estate must be sold to raise money to go on running the rest of it.'

'No.'

Sir Robert moved the papers he held in his hand. He had to have his wife's signature before this necessary sale could be made. He was angry at her refusal, but he was not really surprised; nor did he allow himself to become impatient. He knew that she would have to sign, in the end – and she knew it too.

The book she had been reading fell unnoticed to the floor when at last she rose to her feet and said: 'Then we sell. Then I sign.'

The next morning the head housemaid found her Ladyship's book on the floor in the library and a lamp that had burned out and smoked. She reproved Ernest, the footman, who referred her to Mr Mark, who said that Sir Robert had made himself personally responsible for putting out the lamps. Walter Mark added that in his opinion there had been the usual money troubles last night.

3

In the ordinary course of things, most children do not lead adventurous lives; and the Hatton children were no exception. Their adventures were the ones they made for themselves – deliberately or by accident – and their adventures never really took them beyond home-ground. But home-ground was very large, and a good deal of it dangerous.

To begin with, there was the Hall itself. They knew in which parts – and at which times – to run and laugh; where to keep silence and to tiptoe. There were enemies and half-enemies. Nearly all the servants were on their side, from Walter right down to the odd man who went through the refuse bin by the kitchen hatch for pickings for himself and his Christmas pig. But Lady Hatton's French maid, Hortense, was a spy and an informer; and Mrs Ashley, the cook, although entirely British, must not be crossed in her own kitchen. She had been known to chase with a saucepan a kitchen-maid who overboiled the vegetables or did not wash up fast enough. She had a weakness for Hugh, but had once reported Laura for taking flour dough for their fishing. At the time Mrs Ashley had been preparing to dish up for a large luncheon party.

So the children kept clear of the kitchen; and they were wary of any part of the house where their father might be. They slipped like shadows past his study door. They never set foot inside it unless commanded. Sir Robert had favourite topics upon which he liked to lecture them. He lectured all four on the continuous and crippling cost of their up-keep. Separately, he lectured Tom on the expense of his education and his lack of gratitude; Hugh, on his idleness, which would end in his breaking stones on the road for a living; Laura, on the unlikelihood of her making a good marriage.

To Margaret he said nothing: his ignoring of her might have been the worst of all, except that Margaret was always glad to escape notice of any sort.

The study was lofty, but gloomy and narrow. It had several uncomfortable chairs in it, for this was where Sir Robert conducted estate business, interviewing the agent, the tenants, and the family solicitor. His desk occupied most of the width of the room and faced the window. None of the children on their affairs outside ever allowed themselves to cross his line of vision. Even in his absence they would avoid that particular area of the gravelled court.

They moved about more freely in the gardens, especially among the shrubberies of the wilderness and among the trees, at ground-level or much higher. The giant cedar of Lebanon was their refuge.

Beyond the gardens stretched the great park and the woodlands, with friends such as Dan Power. This territory was bounded by an encircling fence, three miles long, according to Dan, and beyond it lay the tenanted farms and the village of Stanford itself.

There was a certain amount of quiet coming-and-going across the park boundary, where a loose fence-paling could be moved aside or where a tree swept convenient branches over it. The village children came wooding – gathering sticks for their mothers' fires. And Victor came.

It was in this border-country that the children of the house had first met Victor properly. He was birds'-nesting, and they were on the same kind of expedition. They stared up into the tree where Victor was unsteadily perched; he looked hardily down at them. A hostility might have grown up, if Victor had not fallen out of the tree upon them all. His nose bled over Margaret's dress, and the excitement of both staunching the flow and trying to wash out the stain brought them together. Contrary to first expectations, they found that they liked each other.

Victor was different from the village children, as well as

28

different from themselves. His clothes were much mended but at least his own; the village children, on the other hand, generally wore the discarded clothes of their parents – tattered coats and trousers and dresses cut down roughly to fit a youth and smallness for which they had never been intended, and boots too big for them.

In manner, too, Victor was unafraid; his interest in things was an evident curiosity. His family had come from London so that his father might be the schoolmaster at Stanford (and behind the baize door they said that Mr Tomlin had come only so that Evie might have country air). Tom referred to Victor as a townee, but added fairly that he was a townee very quick to learn. He wanted to learn about trees (and how to avoid falling out of them) and birds and their nests and eggs and the fish in the Teal – about everything. At first the children of the house enjoyed the feeling of being experts, oracles; later, they were as equals. Victor became a friend – a secret and occasional friend, of course.

Now, at the beginning of the holidays, Hugh had hoped for more of Victor's companionship. But Tom, with some new idea in his head, dismissed the suggestions of others.

Laura had said: 'Let's walk across the park and through the side gate towards Rampton. There's a field where we might find mushrooms.'

'Too early,' said Tom.

Then Hugh had said: 'We might see Victor. He's sometimes playing about with the other village boys.'

Tom frowned. 'He's very young.'

Hugh said: 'He's only a little younger than I am.'

Tom said: 'He's a lot younger than me.'

'Do you know,' Laura said, 'the Sunday before last, when we were in church and Victor was coming in with the choir, Hugh made animal heads at him with his fingers, and Victor nearly burst out laughing!' In spite of his youth, Laura liked Victor: after all, he was the only friend, boy or girl, that they had.

Margaret said: 'And I wish I could play with Evie. I wish we could invite them both down to the house to play with us.'

Tom laughed at her innocence. 'Mama would have a fit; and I know Papa thinks their father is giving everyone in the village the wrong ideas because he wants the boys and girls to better themselves; and Papa says Victor doesn't touch his cap as he should.'

There was a bleak silence. Then Tom coughed and said, 'As a matter of fact, I thought we might walk to Honeford: there's a boy I know who lives there.' They heard him with amazement. 'He's at school with me. His father and mother came last term and took him out to tea and asked me too.'

'What did you have to eat?' Margaret asked enviously.

Laura brushed this aside. 'Go on, Tom.'

'They were awfully nice. They said they hoped I'd drive over and see them, as I lived quite near. I didn't like to say I couldn't.'

'Are they very grand?'

'No. They said they had quite a small house; they hoped I would not find it very small after living in such a big one.'

'What's the boy like?'

'He's just my age. Not a bit like us; he doesn't hunt or shoot, but he has a bicycle.'

'A bicycle of your own instead of having to ride a horse!' This was Hugh. 'If we all had bicycles, we could go miles and miles away together, anywhere.'

'I'd like being able to go far,' said Laura. 'But all the same, I'd rather ride a horse than a bicycle.'

'I wouldn't,' said Margaret. 'You never know what it's going to do. When you least expect it, they stop and buck and shy and –'

'Look!' said Tom. 'Are we going?'

Under his leadership they set off. At first they talked among themselves. Then Laura and Hugh fell silent, trying to imagine the experience that lay ahead of them. Only Margaret prattled on.

'Won't they be surprised to see all of us, instead of just you! And when they hear that we've walked all the way – but they'll guess, because of the dustiness. Will they have a good tea for us, Tom? Might they be out? If they are, perhaps their servants would give us some tea anyway. Will the boy expect to be asked back? Or have you explained to him about Papa's thinking that kind of thing is wasteful of money?'

But in the end even Margaret stopped talking. All four of them were trudging along in road-dust and hot sunshine, silent.

Suddenly Tom said: 'It's too far.'

'We're not tired,' Laura said. 'Are you?'

'Of course not,' said Tom angrily. 'But look at Meg – she's too little to go all that way –'

'If we have a good tea,' Margaret began, 'and a rest –'

But Tom pulled out his nickel watch from his pocket and said, 'We haven't time. We should be missed at home. We should get into a row.'

'I'd rather go on,' Margaret said, 'even if I am tired, and have Tom's friend's tea.' Hunger made her stubborn.

'No,' said Tom, 'we must go back.' He added cunningly, 'But we might go back by Mrs Dillworth's.' Mrs Dillworth kept the little village shop which sold – among many other things – sweets. The trouble was that none of the children had any money with them.

Tom considered tactics. It was unthinkable to ask Mrs Dillworth outright for anything. On the other hand, she was a kind old woman with a soft spot for Tom, whom she did not often see since he had begun going away to school. It was agreed that the other three should go slowly on while Tom called on Mrs Dillworth.

He walked boldly into the shop and the tinkle of the bell brought the old woman from the back where she had been busy. She threw up her hands in surprise and pleasure.

'Oh!' she cried. 'Master Tom! I hardly recognize you – you've grown into such a fine young gentleman. Now can I get you anything?'

'No, thank you. I just thought I would call and see you as I was passing. The other three have gone on, and I shall have to catch up with them. We mustn't be late home; so I can't wait.' He eyed the big tins that lined the shelf behind the counter and the large glass bottles on the counter itself.

'You must have a bull's eye,' said Mrs Dillworth, 'for it was kind of you to call in and see an old woman. I've never forgotten when you were a little boy and you came up to me and took my hand because you said I might fall on the ice across the stable yard. I'd been down to the big house with a parcel the carrier had left here by mistake. Oh, I remember!'

Tom was smiling, partly at what Mrs Dillworth was saying, partly at the busy way in which her hands moved among the tins and bottles.

'A bull's eye,' said Mrs Dillworth, 'and a bar of chocolate; but I can't forget your brother and sisters.' She dropped four penny bars into a bag and held them out to Tom, with the bull's eye. He reached over the counter, and she gave him a kiss. Blushing, Tom said, 'Good-bye, and thank you so much, Mrs Dillworth.'

He overtook the others soon after leaving the shop, and they stopped to face him eagerly.

'Did you get anything?'

'One bull's eye, and this.' He held up the paper bag in triumph.

'Sweets!'

'Better: chocolate!' He gave them a bar each, reserving the bull's eye. The others recognized his right to dispose of it as he thought fit. In fact, Tom had already decided to keep it for an emergency of hunger among them – although a bull's eye was difficult to divide. Perhaps it would be best to offer it as a gift to Walter, who had a sweet tooth.

Their chocolate lasted almost until they reached the park gate. Here Tom stopped them all. 'Don't forget. It's always here at the beginning of each holidays that we make our wishes. Let's all look west to the setting sun; and don't say anything about your wishes until they've been made.'

The four stood in silence. Then Tom shuffled his feet as a sign that the wishing was over, and Hugh said: 'My wish is always the same wish.'

'Not to have to go into the Navy or the Church,' Laura said sympathetically. These were the two careers considered particularly suitable for second sons at Stanford.

'That's it,' said Hugh. 'But I would like to be grown up as quickly as possible, and be free to travel and explore.'

'I'd like to grow up and *do* something, too,' said Laura, 'not just be married off. But in the end I'd like to marry and have children, mostly boys, and I'd like to live in a big house with big gardens and a park and farms – '

'It sounds like Stanford,' said Tom.

' – And I'd like to manage it, and my husband would rely on my judgement in running it, and we'd make all the farms and so on pay well, so that we had plenty of money, and we'd ride splendid horses and give splendid parties, and go to parties too, and all my children would have lots and lots of friends.'

'Now you, Meg,' said Tom.

'I don't think I want to marry and have children. That always sounds a worry. But I'd have lots and lots of pets – four dogs and two cats. And I'd want you all to live near so that we could visit every day.'

At this the others exclaimed, 'Of course!'

Now for Tom.

He hesitated. 'I'm a bit like Hugh: I know most what I don't want to be, and that is, like Papa. But I think my real wish is to be a soldier and have adventures like the soldiers who went to the South African War.'

They all looked at Tom in silence, and Hugh said, 'You might be killed.'

'No,' said Tom, 'I should have to take care I shot the enemy before he saw me. But I'd like to do something really brave.'

'You're brave already, Tom,' said Margaret.

'No,' said Tom. 'You think I am. I know the times when I'm not brave, even when you think I am.' He spoke fiercely, and his tone forebade questioning. 'So I'd like to be a soldier and then I'd have to try to be brave and I'd know if I succeeded and everyone else would know, and they'd be right.'

After a respectful pause, Hugh said, 'And what about when you inherit Stanford?'

'I'd make great changes. Everywhere there'd be brightness and lots going on; I'd shut up the rooms where we've been unhappy, like Papa's study. And if I couldn't afford to live in Stanford in my way, then I might sell it.'

'Don't ever let Mama know you think of that,' said Laura.

'Of course not. But anyway I wish for a lot of money.'

'A rich wife,' said Margaret.

'I know about that. But perhaps I'd love someone who was poor, and then I'd marry her. But, anyway, if there was enough money to live properly at Stanford, I'd like you all to live with me, or to live very, very near.'

'Yes,' said Laura; Hugh nodded; Margaret beamed. This had always been understood between them.

'Come on, then,' said Tom; and the party turned in at the park gate, making directly for home.

4

THAT night Tom said, 'Tomorrow we must all be up early. Five sharp.' That meant he had planned something. Margaret was unthinkably delighted; Hugh and Laura felt anxiety.

For Hugh, Tom was a little too adventurous sometimes; too brave and reckless. There was that time when Hugh had been sent to climb over the three-storied roof and down a drainpipe from which he had nearly lost his grip. All just to see what bird had built its nest in the cup of the pipe; and it had been only a starling, to Tom's disappointment. On the whole Hugh admitted to himself that he felt safer on expeditions with the girls by themselves. But, of course, he was Tom's man to the death, just the same.

The same went for Laura – very nearly always. But there had been occasions when Laura dug in her toes. Mulishly she then repeated: 'No. I'm the eldest, and I should get the blame for it. No.'

'They wouldn't be as hard on you as on me,' Tom would say. 'Papa prefers you to me; and anyway you're a girl.'

'I wish I weren't. I wish I were a boy. I wouldn't mind then; but as it is – No.' From this she could never be budged; and Tom would have to laugh and say, 'Come on then – let's do something else!'

This time, however, Tom started most acceptably. He said that he wanted to carry out two plans, and the first was to raid the kitchen garden. The children never seemed to have quite enough to eat in the schoolroom or under their parents' eyes in the dining room, so that any expedition for food was of interest to them. Like a guerilla band, they reckoned to live partly off the country.

The door into the kitchen garden was kept locked, but

there was a suitable ladder in a shed at the back of the stables. It was twelve feet long, which Tom said was enough to reach to the top of the wall.

The four children spaced themselves out along the ladder, each at a rung; then together they lifted it and walked in procession down the drive that led to the back gate and the kitchen garden. No window overlooked this drive; and in any case it was early for anyone to be about – even for Phillips, the head gardener, who worked long hours. But as they neared the high wall, Laura asked the time of Tom, as the only one with a watch.

'Five-fifteen.'

'Then that's all right, for the garden door isn't opened until six. But we should be quick because of Phillips.'

'Are you frightened of Phillips?'

'No, but we mustn't get him into trouble. He's kind. Don't you remember when he invited us to tea last year?'

'Yes,' said Margaret, 'and Mrs Phillips said to Hugh, "Help yourself." Mama would never have said that.'

'And I did help myself,' Hugh said reminiscently. 'And a little later, when I was resting, she said it again.'

But Tom's mind was on the present. 'Oh, come on with that ladder. Lift. Push it up –' They did as they were told.

The ladder was in position, and Tom had adjusted it finically. 'Yes. That'll do. Now, Hugh, up you go and make sure there's no one about.'

Hugh went up and looked over the wall. There it all lay below him – a paradise of fruit: strawberry beds and raspberry canes and currant bushes and gooseberry bushes and netted espaliers bearing peaches and apricots and hothouses where grapes and melons and pineapples grew. And not a human being in sight.

Hugh gave the all-clear, but added worriedly: 'There's a tremendous drop on the other side of the wall, you know.'

'Easy,' said Tom. 'We go up, one by one, and sit along the top, and then pull the ladder up and over. Easy.'

They managed this operation, although it was far from easy and ended – something they had not foreseen – in the ladder's standing on its head in the kitchen garden. Some ladders do not have heads, but this one had, since it was wide at the bottom and tapered to the top. The construction was so designed to make the ladder stand particularly steadily on its wide base; but when the ladder stood on its narrow head, with its wide base in the air, the result was a particular amount of unsteadiness.

'I'll hold it firmly from on top, while you three go down,' said Tom. 'And then you three will all have to hold it like anything at the bottom while I come down.'

All four reached the ground sagely and the ladder still stood in position. 'But how shall we get it up again, and sit astride, and pull it up again and over and –'

Tom interrupted Hugh. 'No, no. That's not my idea. The garden door's locked from this side, but the key's left in the lock. So we get out that way. And now we must be quick about the fruit.'

'Let's not bother with gooseberries,' said Laura. 'Mama will let us have some on Sunday, anyway.'

'Peaches then,' said Tom, 'and apricots. About four each. And be careful not to tear the nets. Then all reassemble at the ladder.'

This they did in a few minutes, their pockets now heavy with fruit.

'Smoke's beginning to come out of Phillips's chimney. He must be up.'

'Be quick then.' They brought the ladder down, set themselves to it as before, carted it to the door, unlocked the door, and went through – all still unobserved. Margaret was giggling with nervous relief at being on the safe side of the door again.

'But we can't lock the door behind us!' Laura exclaimed.

'That doesn't matter,' said Tom. 'We've closed it properly.

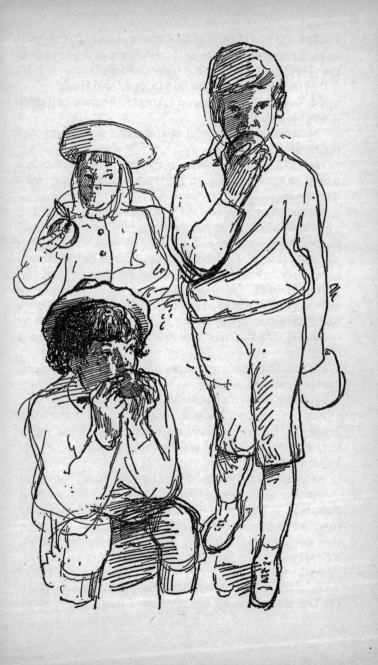

Phillips will just think that he forgot to lock it last night. If he notices our footmarks, he'll think some of the boys from the village got in through the unlocked door.'

'We oughtn't to get them into trouble,' said Hugh.

'Of course not. Phillips won't report it, because he'll think it was his own fault.'

The others were doubtful of this, but Tom pooh-poohed their fears of some discovery.

The ladder was put away again and the three children retired to the shrubbery to eat their fruit and hear Tom's second plan of adventure.

'I have often suspected – ' Tom's pause was impressive. ' – I have often suspected there may be an underground passage connecting our well with the river.'

'I don't think so,' Hugh said flatly. At once he saw himself being made to explore this possibility.

Tom frowned. 'Anyway, we can but try it. After all, you can see a sort of arch and a hole in the side of the well wall. And I have this strong feeling that the well was somehow connected with the river hundreds of years ago. As a means of escape.'

The word 'escape' caught the imagination of the others; but they still had doubts.

'I suppose the well's bottomless?' Hugh asked.

'No. I tested it with a pole recently. It's only about ten feet deep. There's a step-ladder in the shed that would do for the job, and there's an old tea-chest there, too.'

'An old tea-chest?'

'As a boat for the one who does the exploring.'

Together with this ladder and this tea-chest, they all assembled a little later round the well. Tom took the cover off and they peered down. Certainly there was some kind of shadowed archway in one side, partly below water-level.

'Well?' said Tom.

The other three were now studying the wooden tea-chest. The box was obviously too small for Laura or Tom; Hugh might have managed to squeeze into it; but Margaret was the one it would really fit. Even Margaret had to recognize the truth of this.

'Will it sink?' she asked.

'No,' said Tom. 'And I'll be there. I'll go down the ladder first with the chest and be there to help you into it, when you come. Then, with this piece of wood as a paddle, all you have to do is to paddle through the arch and see if it leads to a passage and where the passage leads to.'

Margaret was naturally timid, but the other two seemed hardly more enthusiastic. They stood round in silence; their wish that the plan might be abandoned seemed almost audible.

But Tom was deaf to suggestion. 'I'll start things,' he said, and put the ladder in position and carried the tea-chest down it – with some difficulty, as there was hardly room for the ladder, the chest, and himself. But he managed it, and floated the chest.

'Now, Meg,' he called.

Rather pale, Margaret descended the ladder, with Tom's hands guiding her feet. When she reached him, he pulled her gently sideways into the box-boat.

Margaret gave one of her low screams. 'Hold me – hold the box!'

'You're all right,' said Tom. 'Calm yourself. Don't move until I give you the paddle.'

'I can't move, anyway. It would over-balance the box.'

'You're all right, Meg. Now take the paddle; and at the same time hold the end of this ball of string. The string's your lifeline: I can pull you in with it, if you do get into difficulties.' Then, without waiting to hear more from Margaret, Tom gave the box-boat a strong push with his foot towards the mysterious archway.

'Oh – oh – oh – oh—' Margaret was saying; but whether the exclamations were at what she beheld or at the behaviour of the boat they could not tell, until she became more specific: 'Oh – oh – oh – I'm sinking!'

'Hang on to the string!' Tom called, and pulled. Somehow the life-line was not as effective as might have been expected; but, with a great effort on the part of both, Tom reached out and grasped Margaret's outstretched arm just as the tea-chest filled with water and sank from view; meanwhile, Margaret had got one hand and one foot on the ladder. Within less than a minute they were both safely out of the well again.

Margaret was drenched from the waist downwards, and crying. 'Whatever shall I do? I'll get caught.'

'No,' they all said. 'We will protect you.'

Tom added: 'The important thing is: what did you see?'

Through her crying she got out, 'There is a passage for a little way. It goes right back underground. But then it stops.'

Tom said, 'That doesn't mean there isn't a further escape-route to the river. It may be an underwater one. In fact, if there's an escape-route, then it must go underwater. We have discovered an underwater escape-route.'

For a moment, although they knew in their hearts that Tom's escape-route was not for them, the other three – even Margaret – were dazzled by his achievement. Only Tom could have conceived of such an ambitious project; only he could have worked out the practical details. His fatal weakness, however, was an inability to allow for any degree of failure. Failure caught him out in a particular way.

Here and now, like Failure personified, stood Margaret, steadily streaming with well-water and tears.

The tea-chest had to be left below in the well, together with a ball of string and paddle-shaped piece of wood; but the ladder was hauled up and put back where it came from, and the cover of the well replaced.

Then they rallied to Margaret. After all, Hugh had been almost as wet after the punting expedition, and he had been smuggled indoors with total success. Surely they could manage the same for Margaret.

Margaret's entry was indeed made unchallenged: all seemed to have gone well. But the time was a little later than after the punting expedition, and more people were about than William Kemble, Walter Mark, and the other friends of the children of the house. The children did not see the face that observed them attentively from one of the upper windows. Hortense, their mother's personal maid, noted that the children were out of doors, where they had no business to be at this hour; and she noted among them the dank and dripping figure of Margaret.

Meanwhile, in the kitchen garden, Phillips had discovered that he seemed to have forgotten to lock the garden door the previous night; yet he was a careful man. He was also an intelligent one, and paused long over the strange, deep marks left by the pressures of the wrong end of a tapered ladder. These interested him as much as the bold footprints of the fruit-robbers.

5

'DID you see the state Miss Margaret was in?' said Ernest to Elsie, in the butler's pantry.

'I did that. They wanted me to take her wet clothes to dry by the kitchen fire; but I told them they must get Mrs Ashley on their side first. I didn't want to get across her, for her Ladyship believes everything she says. I would have been risking the sack.'

'You like it here?'

'Yes, when all the children are at home.'

'I've noticed your playing leapfrog with them when no one's about.'

'It reminds me of home. We used to play leapfrog down the back streets with the other kids in our row.'

'Yes. I've noticed your playing with them, especially when Master Tom's home. You cool off me then.'

'No, I don't.' Elsie came close to Ernest and put her arms round his waist, laying her head on his footman's silver-buttoned waistcoat. 'But Tom he's so kind. Always asks after my mum and dad; wants to know how we live at home. I daren't tell him, because a young gentleman couldn't understand. My dad's a miner, and often out of work. We live rough.'

'Ah,' said Ernest. His mother had been a head-housemaid, and one of his grandfathers had been a butler. He knew only the ways of the gentry and of their servants.

'Last holidays,' Elsie confided, 'Master Tom caught me doing the grates. I was black all over; the print dress her Ladyship gave me Christmas was filthy. He says, "You do this every morning of your life while we're lying in bed. I hate to think of it." He says, "One day when I inherit I'll change a lot of things." Then I dream all night

44

that one day I'll be a lady with fine clothes and a carriage.'

Ernest frowned. 'That's folly, my girl.' Then he softened again. 'I got a notice from Hunt's, the agent's, the other day. One situation I would not have minded, as first footman to Lord Caudle: thirty-six pounds a year; two shillings a week beer money; and two shillings a week washing.'

'You would be a millionaire! Why don't you take it?'

'Because I'm waiting to see what you're going to do, Elsie.'

'Then you'll have to wait a good bit. I ain't fourteen yet.'

At this point Walter Mark entered his pantry. 'Clear out of here, Elsie; and you, Ernest, get on with the washing-up of the silver. You're all behind with it.' Some kind of worry made him brusque.

Ernest dared to say respectfully, 'You look upset, Mr Mark.'

'I am. Her Ladyship and Sir Robert are in an uproar about the kids going down the well.'

Elsie was horrified. 'Mrs Ashley told on them, after all!'

'No. It was that Hortense. And now I'm blamed for not hearing them leave the house this morning, and Sir Robert says I'm not worth my keep if burglars could get in as easy as *they* could get out; and I says, "Sir Robert" – keeping my temper, but how I would have liked to have hit him! – "Sir Robert, Master Tom has high spirits." But he pays no attention to that.'

It seemed that Sir Robert had not only scorned Walter's opinion but had been prepared to interfere with his powers. He had said: 'A padlock must be put upon the back door, and I will keep the key.'

'Very well, Sir Robert,' Walter Mark had assented with the utmost correctness. 'And shall I come and get it from you to unlock the door in the morning, when that is necessary?'

'I suppose so. At what time must you open the back door?'

'Mr Phillips is usually the first caller, but sometimes the cowman comes at five with the milk. The postman's cart is early, too, in summer.'

The expression on Sir Robert's face had been such that Walter Mark had had to turn a laugh into a cough and say, 'Beg pardon, sir.'

'The milk could be left outside,' Sir Robert had decided.

'What about the post? Sometimes there may be important letters.'

'True.'

'Then shall I call you at five a.m. for the key, Sir Robert?'

There had been a long silence while Sir Robert paced his study. Finally he said, 'When I get the padlock, I think it better if *you* keep the key.'

'Very good, Sir Robert.'

This had been an outstanding victory for Walter, apparent even in his dry account to Elsie and Ernest.

'Well done, Mr Mark!' Elsie cried admiringly; and Ernest added. 'You got the better of him there, Mr Mark.'

'Maybe,' said Walter gloomily. 'But that's not much help to the four of them at present.'

The row over the well adventure raged all the morning and part of the afternoon. It became clear, however, that Sir Robert was not after all going to carry out his threat of hiring tutors to keep his children's noses to grindstones even during their holidays. Economy seemed the likeliest reason for his holding back. Economy, as Tom pointed out, would explain not only his not hiring tutors but also his telling Hugh that, as a punishment, he would not be sent to school with Tom in the coming autumn, but in the following spring. 'A term's school fees saved,' said Tom, wagging his head.

Their mother had not joined in the storming. Walter re-

47

ported that she was sorry for it all; thought the children had not meant any harm; considered that they had been punished enough by the dreadful realization that Margaret might well have been drowned; and pointed out that they had otherwise begun the holidays with perfect behaviour.

Late in the afternoon the children decided to ask their mother's permission to leave the schoolroom and the house to walk by the river. Surely such exercise might be allowed.

This was the time when their father was usually at work in his study, writing letters and interviewing employees. The children waited and watched until they saw Walter show William Kemble into the study; then they tiptoed downstairs to the drawing-room, where they knew their mother would be.

She smiled when she saw them. 'I was just about to ring the bell to ask Walter to find out what you were doing. For I think we will go out – it's such a lovely evening. We might all go to the kitchen garden. Phillips would like to see you, Tom; he is always asking after you when you are at school.'

There was nothing to be said but, 'Yes, Mama.'

'I thought you might all like to have some gooseberries too. They won't last much longer.'

The four children walked beside their mother to the kitchen garden with a common anxiety; but they had no chance of consulting together for an instant before the crisis – if there were to be a crisis – came upon them.

Tom was the calmest. He carried the conversation with their mother, knowing how to please her. As they walked, he exclaimed at the beauty of the Hall in the afternoon glow. He praised the gardens and the parkland, and showed the keenest interest in everything at Stanford.

'I hear Papa is selling the pineapples,' said Tom with an air of anxiety.

'Yes, and I think it is a great mistake. He gets really

48

nothing for them, since horrid pineapples are now being imported from abroad. Common people don't know the difference between our pineapples and the foreign ones; and they make the same price, ridiculously. Papa says at least it goes towards paying for the heating of the greenhouses.' She sighed. 'In your grandfather's day we had all the fruit for the house. When there was a party, everyone said there was not a pineapple, melon or peach to beat the ones grown at Stanford.'

'I should love to taste one,' said Tom.

'When Papa is away I will tell Phillips to send a pineapple down to the house. One that is a little bruised, of course.'

Tom had certainly put their mother into a good humour by the time they reached the kitchen garden. Innocently they all trooped in by the door through which they had passed in such very different circumstances earlier that day. To their relief, Phillips was not in sight. What luck!

'Now, children, you may have five minutes under the gooseberry nets. Then you must come when I call you.'

They ran to the well-known spot, able for the first time to have private conversation.

'Marvellous!' Hugh said to Tom. 'I mean, the way you said just the right things to please Mama.'

'I didn't know the pineapples were being sold,' said Laura. 'How did you know, Tom?'

'Papa wrote me one of those long boring letters about everything being so expensive and nothing paying. He wants to cut down on the kitchen garden. There are five gardeners, and two do nothing but the hot-houses. He said he couldn't persuade Mama to get rid of the pineapple and melon houses, but at least they were selling the fruit.'

Margaret was not interested in all this but, her mouth full of gooseberries, asked, 'Suppose Phillips comes? And suppose – ?'

At that moment they heard their mother call. They looked up and saw her with the head gardener. They put the gooseberry nets back into place and walked slowly to the waiting two.

'Phillips says somebody – or rather, some people – got into the kitchen garden last night or very early this morning, and stole a quantity of apricots and peaches.'

Phillips looked steadily at the four silent children and said, 'In fact, they did not take very much of the fruit. I think I may have disturbed them, for I was about soon after five o'clock. The marks were fresh then.'

Lady Hatton said, 'If the thieves were boys from the village – '

'No, my lady, I think it unlikely that any boys from the village are to blame.'

'Oh!' said Lady Hatton, puzzled. But she knew that Phillips was very reliable in his judgement.

'I did not report the theft to Sir Robert this morning, my lady, because so little was taken, as I've said, and because we can't sell the fruit this year, anyway. There's a glut.'

'As long as this pilfering does not happen again, Phillips.'

'I think it will not, my lady. From all appearances the incident occurred because an under-gardener failed to lock the door last night. At least, it was found unlocked this morning.'

'The man should be reprimanded.'

'Yes, my lady; but in fact he probably relied on my checking the door. I always do it.'

'You failed to check that the door was locked?'

'I did check, my lady, but unaccountably failed to realize it had been left unlocked.'

'That certainly must not happen again, Phillips.'

'No, my lady.'

The children listened aghast to the latter end of this conversation. They knew that Phillips had the greatest devotion and respect for their mother, having known her all her life, and served her family for all his own. (His feeling for Sir

Robert, who sold his pineapples and tried to raze his hot-houses, could also be shrewdly estimated.) But even the most devoted servant does not enjoy being reproved for a fault he did not commit; nor should he be expected to endure it.

Laura had flushed; Hugh was twisting his fingers together in a kind of agony; even Margaret's eyes and mouth made three pitiful O's. And Tom naturally became their spokesman: 'Mama,' he said over-loudly, 'we think you should know – '

Quickly but not rudely Phillips interrupted him. 'I know what Master Tom is going to say, and the rent in the gooseberry net is being mended within the hour.'

He pointed to one end of the gooseberry net and Lady Hatton's gaze went obediently in that direction. But Phillips did not look that way, nor the children: they looked at each other. And while the children looked, they saw Phillips close one of his intelligent eyes in a wink.

The children left the kitchen garden with no further stain upon their characters, and walked back to the house with their mother. Their father was still preoccupied in his study.

The day ended more peacefully and with more repletion – because of the gooseberries – than might have been expected. Alone in the nursery again, they relaxed. Only Margaret, who was always the slowest in any guessing game, failed to appreciate what Phillips had done for them.

Tom declared: 'He's a true sport'; and Laura agreed.

Hugh simply said: 'What you'd expect from someone married to someone who says "Help yourself".'

6

THE raid for fruit had turned out to be something upon which the children could congratulate themselves, after all. Quite differently, the well adventure brought them into ridicule as well as disgrace. Their father raged against the idiocy of Tom's supposition almost as much as against their disobedience ('But he never told us beforehand not to put Meg in a tea-chest down the well!') and their general wickedness. Even Lady Hatton, with her intimate knowledge of Stanford and its history, shook her head decisively at the idea of any secret escape-way.

The escape-way had vanished as a practical thing; yet the idea of it seemed to have rooted itself in their minds. That night the dreams of three of them – Margaret never dreamed – were of escape.

'That huge sword that hangs high up in the great hall,' Tom began, ' – you know, it was Sir Thomas Stanford's, that fought for Charles the First – '

'Yes,' said Laura.

'No,' said Hugh. 'No, no, no. I mean, I don't believe we could get it down, and we should never be able to get it back.'

'In my dream,' Tom said emphatically, 'I climbed up the wall by the palms of my hands and the soles of my bare feet.' He looked hard at Hugh. 'Very easily.'

'Do go on, Tom,' said Laura.

'I took the sword and waded through our underwater way that doesn't exist, and I waved the sword and shouted my war cry: "A Stanford! A Stanford!" '

'Mama would have been pleased,' said Hugh.

'And Papa would have been furious,' said Laura.

'Were they about?' Margaret asked, puzzled.

But Tom had been alone. His charge had brought him out of the well-tunnel and up – quite unexpectedly – into South Africa, where the war was still going on after all. He had joined in at once with his sword and – as far as he could tell in the mingled confusions of battle and dream and torrid heat – had particularly distinguished himself.

In Laura's dream the tunnel had been much loftier, and she had escaped down it on horseback, astride, not side-saddle, because William Kemble had said positively: 'It's the only way, Miss Laura.' And Hugh had escaped on the huge silver tea-tray from Walter Mark's pantry, and had expected to pick Victor up as shipmate from the wooded river-bank where they had last seen him. Then Victor and Hugh would have sailed downstream, carried unerringly by the current, down to the sea, and across it . . .

'Only Victor hadn't turned up by the time I woke,' said Hugh.

Waking or dreaming, Hugh would have liked to seek Victor out again; but Tom and Laura both hesitated now. They pointed out that they hardly dared risk another row like the one over the well adventure. For the rest of the holidays they must be good. Or at least they must ensure there was not the slightest possibility of their parents' discovering any trace of badness.

Submissively they gave themselves up to the ordering of their parents. Nearly every day they rode out, of course, either with their father or with William Kemble. Laura was the only one who enjoyed these rides, whatever the company; but, on the other hand, she had regularly to suffer being taken out in the carriage in the afternoon to pay calls with her mother. Laura had to wear her best clothes and be driven for miles and miles and nobody ever seemed at home anyway, and certainly they never got any tea.

Often the children fished, which was a sport of which their parents approved. Their mother liked the pretty, pensive scene they made, sitting or standing on the green river-bank, watching their floats; and Sir Robert observed that the amusement was productive. They had only three rods between them, but Margaret did not care for fishing. Conveniently, however, she liked the importance of looking after the bait and never tired of sitting on the bank beside it.

Their companionable silence was broken only by the usual fishing remarks – 'I had a bite,' or, 'Meg, more bait.' The river rippled by; the wood-pigeons cooed sleepily; the sun began to set. Laura said: 'The clock on the gate-house has struck,' and Tom said, 'We must get back.' They pulled in their lines and collected the few bony roach they had caught. They usually divided the catch among their friends beyond the baize door. 'I wish we had more to give them,' said Hugh.

They fished in the evenings. In the daytime they spent a good deal of their free time with Dan Power in the park. They knew at what hour to find him by the rookery on the river-bank setting his traps. His pole would already be hung with couples of dead rabbits, and above, on a tree would be hanging the corpses of jays, jackdaws and stoats. He set them there not only in proof of his industry as a game-keeper, but, as he said, 'as an example to the rascals to keep away. Or I'll shoot 'em.' From this warning carrion, Margaret and even Laura shrank away. But the two boys helped Dan with his trap-setting, and in return he showed them the secrets of the park. He showed them an owl's nest and a kingfisher's tunnel, and they managed to get an egg from each for their collection. Sometimes Hugh looked upwards to the heronries, remembering Victor's boast and Dan's scorn; but he said nothing.

They worked together in their gardens, mainly lettuce-growing and potato-digging; and they went long walks, searching for unripe hazel-nuts and blackberries. As the year began to turn from summer to autumn, Lady Hatton did not pay so many calls, and there were fewer rice-puddings to be delivered to the sick and poor.

Lady Hatton seemed anxious that they should have some fun, and suggested of her own accord that she would play croquet with them and yet once more teach Margaret the way to hold the mallet. When they came to her in the evening, to say their prayers before bed, she would detain them to tell of the past glories of Stanford – how her father, their grandfather, had lived; of the gay parties there had been in the days when money was plentiful; of his great reputation as a sportsman. He had been the best rider to hounds that the Hunt had seen for many a day. On one occasion he had been the first rider at a kill in a nine-mile chase, and, not content with that, had come home to go out again shooting and got a brace of partridge, three pheasants, and a hare – all with only six shots.

Afterwards Hugh said, 'Mama wants you to be like Grandfather, Tom.'

Tom said, 'And if I died, she'd want *you* to be like him.'

'I hope you never, never die,' Hugh said.

Their mother's tone of speech was often regretful, wistful; but they now thought they noticed a new plaintiveness. At the same time their father began to appear unusually cheerful.

'It's because the holidays will soon be over,' Hugh said.

But Walter, consulted as usual, knew more than their parents had thought fit to tell them. 'Sir Robert's going up north with her Ladyship for two nights, to your Grandmama Hatton's house.'

'Oh,' said Laura, 'so that's it.' Sir Robert had inherited the family house in Yorkshire, but could not live in it because of his heavier responsibilities at Stanford; yet his heart was there.

'They're going,' said Walter, 'and leaving you all here – in charge.'

'In whose charge? Yours, Walter?' But they were hardly hopeful of it.

'My goodness, no! In charge of that Hortense – and a precious lot of care she'll contrive to take of you.'

'We'd far rather be uncared for, anyway,' said Laura.

'Yes,' said Tom; and from that single syllable of speech the other three knew that they were to make the most of their freedom.

On the day set for the departure, the four children waited in the great hall for their parents to pass through it. Everyone was waiting. Walter Mark stood with his hand on the door leading to the wing of the house from which they would come. Ernest was at the open front door, a fur rug over one arm. Beyond, the children could see the brougham with William on the box and James Pervis holding open the carriage door.

There was the sound of one pair of feet approaching fast. Walter opened the door of the hall enough to allow Hortense to sweep through. She was carrying Lady Hatton's jewel box, and saying, 'They will be late – they will be late!'

'Don't get into a stew,' said Walter. He pulled out his watch. 'They've plenty of time.'

Hortense disliked the English and particularly disliked their metaphors. 'Stew – stew! You nasty man, it is you English who live on that horrid stew.'

'Better than living on frogs,' said Walter. Immediately after he had said this, he bowed dignified from the waist: in anyone else but a first-class butler, it might have been called doubling up with laughter. Ernest sniggered.

'You are a common man,' Hortense said angrily.

All sound ceased abruptly as two pairs of feet were heard. The three servants drew themselves up; the children turned towards the door, which Walter now opened wide. Sir Robert and Lady Hatton were here.

Lady Hatton kissed each of her children in turn. 'Remember to be good. Don't get into mischief, or soil or tear your clothes, or go outside the park except with Hortense – or

56

with William, of course, when you ride.'

Sir Robert's kisses – on the forehead instead of the cheek – followed their mother's. He paused only at Hugh: 'You must brush that hair out of your eyes. One should be able to see your face.'

All four children had been murmuring, 'Good-bye, Mama – good-bye, Papa,' and now they all said, 'Yes, Papa,' as if the remark to Hugh had applied to them all.

Sir Robert had already turned to Walter. 'My top hat?'

'In, Sir Robert; and your umbrella and her Ladyship's rug. You have one hour and five minutes, which should give the horses comfortable time to the station.'

Sir Robert grunted and moved to the front door. Lady Hatton went before him, her long travelling dress rustling over the floor. Hortense packed her and the dress into the brougham, and Sir Robert followed. Ernest added the rug. James shut the door and in a flash was up on the box as William drove the carriage off at a smart trot.

They were gone; and Ernest had shut the front door, and he and the other two servants had disappeared. The children were left in the great hall, no longer a place for respectful steps and hushed voices.

'Hurrah!' cried Laura, and 'Hurrah – rah – rah!' shouted Tom, running and leaping ahead of them all, beneath the gaze of those centuries of Stanfords; and 'Boo!' said Hugh, stopping abruptly to flap his arms beneath the portrait of Grandpapa Hatton, as if hoping to startle him from his godly expression; and Margaret jumped about with them and laughed till she was sobbing with over-excitement. The sun cast patterns of red, blue, and yellow through the stained-glass windows on to the family portraits, the busts, the suits of armour, and down on to the twirling figures of the children of the house dancing for joy over the marble floor.

7

THE master and mistress of the house had taken a fur rug with them into Yorkshire because the summer lately had been cold – although with few wet days to imprison the children in the house. Now, like a blessing upon those young or carefree enough to enjoy it, a brief heat-wave began.

The children spent the afternoon playing cricket with Walter and Ernest. A jug of lemonade, provided for them by Mrs Ashley and carried out by Elsie, waited under a tree.

Hugh loved cricket – and cricket-talk – without being very good at it; Tom was the one for that. As usual, he tried to show off to Laura as a bowler and cussed her in a man-of-the-world way for not stopping the balls he hit. On other occasions Laura had ended by walking off the field, and no one had been able to persuade her to return. This time, however, Walter was there to keep the peace between them all. He encouraged Laura by praise: 'My! You'd have to go a long way to find a girl who could play as well as that.' Of Margaret he said: 'She's little. Don't you be hard on her, Master Tom, because if you are, I'll bowl fast at you. Very fast.' To Hugh he always said the same kindly thing: 'You're coming on well – coming on well, Master Hugh.'

Walter was a good cricketer and had been tried for the County. With Ernest, he gave them all good practice; then he suggested a match: 'Miss Margaret and Master Hugh and I challenge you others – Master Tom and Miss Laura and Ernest.'

'We'll win!' cried Tom, flushed with exercise and excitement and sun.

Ernest put in respectfully, 'Mr Mark is too good for the likes of us, but, of course, we'll have a try.'

Walter Mark's side won. It was Margaret who hit the

winning run, but Tom said that Laura should not have bowled under-arm at her. Laura did not reply to this, because she could not bowl over-arm.

They finished their lemonade, and the day ended perfectly.

Hortense had not troubled them much, and the next day she was going in the carrier's cart to visit a friend some ten miles away. 'So we'll have most of the day to ourselves,' said Tom. 'Give her ten minutes and then we'll be off.'

'Where to?'

He glanced indulgently at Hugh. 'We really ought to look Victor up.'

Walter, to whom they let fall their intention, told them to be wary of Victor's father. 'It isn't just that your papa and mama don't approve of him: he's taken against Sir Robert and Lady Hatton.'

'*He's taken against them!*' repeated Ernest, who happened to be in the butler's pantry. He was amazed at the daring of the schoolmaster.

'The little girl's being so ill seems to have set him all on edge,' said Walter. 'So I've heard.'

The four children approached the schoolmaster's house with caution. It was only a little bigger and better than the other cottages of the village, and was overshadowed on one side by the church and on the other side by the rectory. The school was a church school.

Skulking round the house, they were able to locate Victor's parents. His mother was at the back of the house, baking in the kitchen. His father was on the church side, scything the long grass of the churchyard – one of the duties of the Stanford village schoolmasters. And on the opposite side of the house, through an open window, they could hear the voice of Victor himself reading aloud – presumably to Evie.

They were about to walk boldly up to this open window, when Laura, glancing at the rectory, saw the Rector, Mr

Prout. He was standing at his study window, staring out. It was impossible to decide whether he was simply in a day-dream or working out a Sunday sermon, or whether he was really watching the schoolmaster's house. Mr Prout was an elderly widower, childless, and unappreciative of children. He had regular interviews with their father on church matters.

They waited for the Rector to withdraw from the window, but he did not. They waited for Victor to come out, but he did not; he went on reading aloud, indoors.

At last Tom said, 'We retreat.'

They began to go sadly homewards under the cruel beat of the sun. They had failed to make contact with Victor, and their plan for the rest of the day was in ruins. For they had intended to get Victor to come with them into the park to climb trees. In particular, they had wanted him to explain to them his plan – Hugh was sure he had one – for climbing the tall trees of the heronry.

They left the village behind, still creeping dispiritedly along, their heads bowed, and it was thus that Hugh saw what he saw. Amazed and awed, he cried, 'Look!'

There it lay, that most unlikely thing in that most un-likely place: a half-crown, shining dimly up from the white dust of the roadway.

They discussed only briefly where it might have come from – to whom it might have belonged. They liked best Laura's suggestion: 'a rich passer-by who will not return.' For there was not the smallest doubt in the world, it was theirs now by right of discovery. It was theirs, and its ownership had changed everything for them, so that the heat of the sun became again the blessing that it had been.

'What shall we buy with it?'

Unexpectedly Margaret was the one who thought fastest: 'Liquorice bootlaces. Sherbet. Aniseed balls. Bull's eyes. Chocolate – bars and drops and – '

'We ought perhaps to think of others,' said Laura. The

other three looked at her anxiously. 'I only mean,' she explained, 'the others that we know and like specially – our favourite friends.'

'Like Walter,' said Hugh.

'And Elsie. She's a sport, too,' said Tom.

'And William,' said Laura.

Margaret gave up without regret the liquorice, sherbet, aniseed balls, bull's eyes and chocolate. She had a generous heart for those she loved. 'But shall we really divide the half-crown among them?'

'No, we'll buy presents for them out of it. That'll be the fun of the thing. We'll go shopping in Honeford this very afternoon, telling nobody.'

'Half-a-crown won't go very far, even for one friend each,' Hugh said.

Tom coughed. 'I have a shilling,' he said, 'left over from last term at school.'

'Are you sure you can spare it, Tom?' Laura asked.

'Yes. Only I shall have to think carefully. You know that Papa never gives me more than he thinks I strictly need, and before he gives me any money for next term, he'll ask to see the accounts for last term. I mustn't show anything left over.'

'You could have spent the shilling on stamps and note-paper.'

'Papa would want to know who I was writing to so often.'

'Fishing tackle,' Hugh suggested. 'Hooks and lines and floats. Papa never fishes, so he doesn't even know what they cost.'

'Right,' said Tom. 'That makes three shillings and six-pence.'

'I still have two silver three-penny bits from the pudding last Christmas,' said Margaret.

'Four shillings,' said Tom. 'We'll take the half-crown home' – Hugh was holding it flat on the palm of his hand –

'and get the other money to add to it. Nobody talk as we go, because we'll think out exactly how to use it all – each choose a favourite friend and decide on the best present for him or her.'

Immediately after lunch they set out on foot for Honeford with a total of four and a penny-halfpenny. The extra penny-halfpenny had been raised by Laura and Hugh – literally raised, from between two floor-boards.

They went by a winding lane, now deep in summer dust, its hedgerows pale with it. From their boots up the children became dustier and dustier – to their satisfaction. 'I don't believe anyone would recognize us – at least, at first sight,' Laura said.

In fact, the only vehicles to pass them were farm carts and a dog-cart or so driven by a farmer or tradesman. No carriages of those gentry who might know Sir Robert and Lady Hatton and – but this was far less likely – know their children.

In Honeford the shops were not many in number, but they included a tobacconist's and barber's in one, which also sold scent, soap, sweets – everything that the heart could wish. They went directly there to buy their presents: tobacco for Walter, a clay pipe for William Kemble, and a packet of Black Cat cigarettes for Phillips. The cigarettes were chosen by Margaret because she liked the picture of the cat on the packet. She might not have chosen to give them to Phillips, but the other three put pressure on her. They felt that they owed it to Phillips since the fruit-raid.

For Elsie, Tom chose a small bottle of violet scent, costing sixpence.

Most gratifyingly, these purchases left them with one and four-pence over. They spent four-pence on sherbet to quench their thirst. 'And that leaves us with exactly a shilling,' said Tom. It was not clear whose shilling this was, so Tom carried it in his pocket for the time being.

This was a dead time of the day and they had seen very

few people – the shopkeeper, an errand boy, an old man with a scythe over his shoulder, a woman pushing a pram laden with firewood and followed by two small children dragging large branches of it.

'You've not seen your friend from school, have you, Tom?' Margaret asked chattily.

'No,' said Tom, shutting up the conversation like a box with a tight-fitting lid.

They had turned homeward, choosing a way slightly different from the one by which they had come. As they went, they sucked up sherbet and perspired.

Ahead of them along this new road they now saw a small mountain of stones, with an old man sitting upon its foothills. He was wearing protective glasses, for he was methodically breaking stone after stone with a hammer.

'Look, Hugh,' whispered Laura. Stone-breaking should naturally be of interest to Hugh, since this was what Papa predicted for him.

As they came up to the stone-breaker, he stopped to greet them: 'Good afternoon, young ladies and gentlemen.'

'Hard work on a hot day,' Tom said kindly.

'No so bad when you can sit to it,' said the old man. 'Without my leg, I need that.' They saw that one of his legs ended in a wooden stump which protruded from his very ragged trousers.

'How long does it take you to break all those stones?' Laura asked.

'Two days of twelve hours each – if it doesn't rain. You can't work so fast in the rain.'

'Do you like it?' Hugh asked.

'Breaking stones?' The old man made a hoarse little sound that was either a dusty laugh or a dusty cough. He went on: 'I liked it better when I was serving the Queen in the army – although I lost my leg then. I lost it in the South African war. I'd go back to the army now if they'd have me. But, of course, they won't.'

'Anyway,' said Laura, looking sideways at Hugh, 'you're doing a very useful job now, I suppose.'

'Oh, yes,' He made the same throaty sound. 'I'm glad to think that I'm making the stones ready to fill the potholes in the road, so that the carriages won't bump about so much. That's bad for the springs of the carriages and for the coach-men and the horses and the fine gentry that ride in the car-riages.' He seemed to be staring at them, but they could not see his eyes properly behind the glasses.

'We must be going on, I'm afraid,' said Tom.

To which the old man replied, 'God bless you,' and returned at once to his hammering.

When they had gone out of earshot, Hugh stopped and said, 'I'd like to give the shilling that's left over to the stone-breaker.'

'Yes,' said Margaret. 'He looked so poor.'

'But we might need it in the future,' said Laura.

'He needs it now,' said Hugh.

Tom sided with Laura, and wondered whether the stone-breaker was deserving: their mother said this should always be taken into consideration in the giving of charity.

Hugh said: 'You didn't wonder whether we were deserv-ing when I found the half-crown.'

Tom began, 'It was quite different when we found the half-crown – '

But Hugh interrupted, 'When I found the half-crown; and it wasn't different.' Clearly he felt very strongly indeed about the stone-breaker: it was seldom that he opposed Tom in this way.

In the end they agreed to toss for it; heads the shilling was given, tails it wasn't. Tossing for it was really Tom's idea, brought from school. He instructed Laura, as the eldest, exactly how to do it – balance the shilling on her thumbnail, and then flip it into the air, to fall and give them their de-cision.

Perhaps remembering Tom's criticism of her as a bowler,

Laura flipped with great suddenness and force: the coin sailed into the air in a wide curve and came down into the tangle of long wayside grass.

The searched desperately, but could not find it.

'There goes our shilling,' said Tom at last.

'His shilling,' said Hugh.

They looked back to the stone-breaker and saw that he had been resting from his work to watch the antics of the young gentry. He called out something to them, but they could not hear what it was; and Tom, suddenly setting off in the direction of home again, said, 'Come *on*!'

They trailed after him.

The giving of the presents, when they reached home, cheered them, however.

Elsie said, 'Oooh!' when she realized that the little bottle of scent was for her. She pulled out the cork for a sniff. 'Oooh! I shall smell like the fine ladies now – but I mustn't let her Ladyship smell me. It's beautiful. I never thought I should ever have a present from you young ladies and gentlemen.' She beamed at them all, but especially at Tom, who had handed the present over.

William Kemble said that a clay pipe was exactly what he needed, as he had just broken his old one. Laura said, 'I chose it.' She wanted to stand well with William because he was such an excellent horseman and could drive a four-in-hand. She wanted to ride and drive as well as he could – these seemed to be the only things that girls could do as well as boys. Better, sometimes.

Phillips was not at home when they called at his cottage, but his wife said that he would be particularly pleased with the cigarettes. She invited them in and offered them slices of bread with butter and raspberry jam, which they did not refuse. Also cups of tea, after which she told their fortunes in the tea-leaves. They all had really splendid fortunes: Tom won the nation's admiration for some great act of valour; and Hugh travelled right round the world; and the girls mar-

ried handsome, rich, kind husbands and lived happily ever after – only Laura asked, 'Is there nothing interesting before that?' and Margaret said flatly that she would not marry – although she had no objection to living happily.

But Walter, naturally, had been the first to have his present. His tobacco was handed to him by Hugh because – although they all liked Walter very much, and relied upon him – Hugh was the one who admired him so tremendously. The gift took Walter by surprise and clearly touched him: 'You went all the way to Honeford and bought this for me with your own money?'

Hugh said, 'Yes, we did.' Then Walter drew Hugh to him and kissed him on the cheek, and did the same for the two girls, and shook Tom by the hand.

Afterwards – after all the presents had been given and they were going to bed in the balminess of the evening of that sun-blest day – Hugh said: 'Walter has a wife somewhere, hasn't he?'

'Yes,' said Laura, 'but no children.'

'I wish we were his children,' said Hugh.

8

THE weather broke as Sir Robert and Lady Hatton came home. The short remainder of the holidays was mostly wet and always overcast. Fräulein Schmidt would soon be back from her home in Germany; she would at once resume lessons with Laura, Hugh and Margaret in the schoolroom. That was a prospect bad enough, but even before that Tom was going back to school. They would be split up again.

They spent the last day of their holidays visiting their old haunts – the places where they had been most happy together.

They said their evening prayers in their mother's presence as usual. Afterwards she said how sorry she was that their summer holidays were at an end, but that Christmas would soon be here. They did not contradict her, but shared a dull amazement. Blackberries and hazel-nuts were still ripening; winter was yet unimaginable. Between them and Christmas lay a desert of eternity.

As they were going upstairs, after leaving their mother, Tom was called into his father's study. Neither sat: Tom remained standing by the door he had just shut behind him; his father paced up and down as he talked.

Sir Robert said that Tom should be grateful to his parents for these holidays at home – for all the comforts and good times he enjoyed. This, said Sir Robert, was a gift of more significance than any pocket-money.

Tom said, 'Yes, Papa.' The amount of pocket-money for the coming term had been very insignificant.

Sir Robert then spoke of the importance of hard work. 'Remember, you live in Stanford Hall, but you are a Hatton – a Hatton.'

'Yes, Papa.'

This one-sided conversation was so familiar to Tom that he needed to listen with only half an ear. In order not to prolong the interview, it was his rule to say nothing, but 'Yes, Papa,' every so often.

'Yes, Papa.'

'And always remember,' Sir Robert was saying, 'that children can show their gratitude to their parents only by their obedience and affection.'

This was the end of the interview.

'Yes, Papa.' Now, after a kiss, he was allowed to leave the study.

He joined the others upstairs in the schoolroom. They should have been going to bed, but they were waiting for him. In an attempt to cheer him they had agreed to begin softly singing *For he's a jolly good fellow* as soon as they saw him, and this they did.

They became aware of approaching footsteps in the passage outside. Their singing died away suddenly. The steps were certainly too light for their father, but might this not be a messenger from their parents – perhaps Hortense? Had Papa and Mama heard them?

Elsie entered with a plate of cakes, and they all burst out laughing.

Elsie said: 'Mr Mark thought he heard singing and told me to slip along and tell you to watch out, or Sir Robert might hear you as he goes in to dinner.'

'But what about the cakes?'

'Mrs Ashley saved them for you, and she's sorry you're going, Master Tom – and so am I.'

'Lovely,' said Margaret. They were all eating. 'We never get a cake.'

'I know that,' said Elsie, 'and I risked my life coming up with them. Goodness – if I got caught!'

'We should protect you,' said Tom.

'I dare say. But you couldn't stop them sending me away;

and there are plenty of girls willing to step into a place like mine.'

'Have a cake, Elsie,' said Tom.

'Thank you, sir; but to tell you the truth, we are better off in the servants' hall than you are here. Mrs Ashley may be a bit fiery, but she's on our side; and what with pooling our handsome – a quarter of tea a week and a pound of sugar is handsome – and what with left-overs from the dining-room – if Ernest don't have a go at 'em first – but even he has to be a bit careful – ' Elsie had got lost in her long speech; she decided to end it. 'Anyway, we're downright sorry for you.'

'Thank you, Elsie,' Laura said with her mouth full, and the others made the same acknowledgement, as far as they happened to be able.

The cakes were excellent, and seemed to go to their heads like wine.

'Do you know who we thought you were?' asked Hugh. 'The Frog!'

Suddenly they had joined hands round Elsie and were dancing and chanting, in senseless joy. 'She's not the Frog – she's not the Frog!'

Then, one idea leading to another in a delightful way: 'Let's play leapfrog!'

At once they broke the circle and rushed out into the passage, where there was the distance they needed, carrying Elsie with them. But Elsie was frightened of an uproar, and of what discovery might follow. She slipped through their fingers and ran giggling down the back stairs.

So the four children played leapfrog by themselves, furiously, as never before, and seemingly careless of the noise they might be making. After all, what worse could happen to them now than Tom's departure tomorrow and Fräulein Schmidt's return the day after?

But, in fact, from long experience, they knew how to play tumultuously and yet quietly – to laugh in a whisper, to fall softly; and before they began, even in their utmost excitement, they had torn off their shoes.

Nobody came to them with a message from the dining-room, where Sir Robert and Lady Hatton now sat at their stately eating, waited upon by Walter and Ernest. Nobody cut short their farewell celebrations. They went to bed at last, tired, dishevelled, happy for the time being. The day had ended better than any of them could have hoped.

Early the next morning Tom set off, his mother going with him as far as the railway station. As the brougham made its way up the back drive, Laura, Hugh and Margaret ran after it.

William did not let the horses go faster than at a slow trot, so that the three children could keep up with the carriage and even put on a spurt and go ahead to open the back gate. As the brougham went through, Tom put his head out of the window to say, 'Good-bye, Laura – Meg – Hugh!' They could see that his eyes were full of tears.

The three stood at the gate calling their good-byes as long as they saw Tom's hand waving from the window. But in a matter of a minute or so the brougham was out of sight.

Then they still stood – in silence, until Margaret burst out: 'How can we go on living without Tom?'

Laura said sternly, 'We must.'

They turned and went slowly back to the house.

9

THEY measured time by their holidays, because then they were together – especially by the summer holidays, with outdoor freedom and length of days. The summer holidays just ended seemed another landmark in the slow journey towards being grown up, towards independence.

Always, at the park gates, when holidays began, Hugh wished 'to be grown up quickly'; and Laura and Tom felt with him. Only Margaret did not particularly long for it. But she wished above all for the companionship of the other three, and therefore their will was hers without question.

There had been landmarks of past holidays, such as – several years ago now – Tom's first return from boarding school; and there were landmarks ahead. Tom would reach the age of thirteen and have to pay full fare on the railway – 'and a fine old dust-up there'll be with Sir Robert when that happens,' said Walter. And because Tom was growing up, he would soon be given a bedroom of his own, and Hugh would sleep alone in the nursery. One by one the children would grow old enough to begin dining regularly with their parents in the evening. None of them would enjoy it.

All this lay ahead. But the children knew that the summer holidays just past were probably the last of a kind. For the last time Hugh had been at home with Laura and Margaret to welcome Tom back from school; but next summer Hugh himself would be away at school. This seemed almost certain from remarks dropped by their parents and noted by Walter and Ernest for report on the other side of the baize door.

'Lucky you,' Laura said to Hugh. 'I know Tom says school is horrid – food worse than at home; canings; chilblains and things. But at least it's escape. Lucky you.'

Hugh made no answer. The three of them were talking in the girls' bedroom, safe as usual while their parents dined below. Laura was moving restlessly from place to place in the room as she talked; she seemed angry, but it would have been difficult to say with whom. Margaret sat placidly listening.

Laura picked up the ebony-backed hand-mirror which had been given to her by her mother on her thirteenth birthday. If the glass had really been intended to help her to grow up into an elegant lady, then it failed in its purpose: Laura would never willingly use it. Now, however, she was glaring into it: 'Laura Hatton,' she said with fierce scorn, and slammed the mirror face downwards upon the top of the dressing-table, so that Margaret jumped.

'You'll have cracked it,' said Hugh; and she had. 'Seven years' bad luck now.'

'What could be worse luck than being Laura Hatton?' Laura asked.

Margaret said: 'Whatever do you mean?'

'I'm a girl. I'm older than Tom, but it's Tom who will inherit Stanford. I'm cleverer than Hugh' – this had always been agreed among them, without vanity on one side or rancour on the other – 'but he's the one to be sent away to school, to be educated properly, so that in the end he can *do* something. I'm a girl; I stay at home; I wait to grow up and be married off.' She ended her outburst as she had begun it, by repeating angrily at Hugh: 'Lucky you to be going away – lucky you – lucky you –'

Suddenly and just as angrily he was shouting: 'Shut up! Shut up, I say!'

Margaret had risen from where she sat, horrified, 'Hush! They'll hear you!'

In the following silence, however, there was no bell-ringing from below, no voice, no footsteps coming to them. All that while Laura had been staring at Hugh, as amazed as if he had turned into a stranger. Now she said quietly: 'You

75

idiot! Now that you have your chance, you're afraid. It's not the canings or the chilblains or anything; it's just the going away, for the first time in your life. The going away. What I'd give anything for. You're afraid of it, after all.'

'Shut up,' Hugh said again.

Margaret was almost crying in her distress: 'What is it? What are you quarrelling about?'

'We're not quarrelling,' said Laura.

'It's nothing you'd understand,' said Hugh, and turned and left the room for his own.

Margaret, who seldom worried about anything, actually lay awake in bed that night. She quivered with a fear for the very ground of her existence – her family: her two brothers and her sister. She had never seen such a quarrel before, or – if it must not be called a quarrel – such bitterness; she was bewildered by it. The distant future that Laura had seen in her hand-glass, the immediate future that Hugh feared and was ashamed of fearing – both would always be beyond her understanding.

Of the four of them, Margaret would always remark least upon the changes of time. For the others, things seemed to happen too slowly at Stanford; for her – if she thought about it at all – they seemed to happen too fast, leaving her further and further behind. She was not growing up as the others were growing up; in some ways she would always be a little girl. 'Not the bright one of the family; only ninepence in the shilling,' they said on the servants' side of the baize door, when none of the children could hear them.

To Margaret, once the quarrel that was not a quarrel had subsided, the time to Christmas passed smoothly enough. She did not mind the dull repeating pattern of meals, walks and lessons with Fräulein Schmidt. She did not envy Hugh his adventures. Since the evenings had drawn in, he found it easy to slip out under cover of darkness to meet Victor. Jet, chained in his kennel by the back door, was the only creature to observe all his comings and goings.

Laura had said she would not go with him on such expeditions; nor would she let Margaret go. She had suddenly said that Victor was Hugh's friend, not theirs.

'But he's a friend of all of us. You liked him.'

'All right. But it's silly to pretend he's not your special friend: you're both boys, and nearly the same age. It's silly to pretend we four can always do everything together, share everything. You're the only one with a friend; the rest of us haven't friends. Tom hasn't made a real friend at school, whatever he says; and Meg and I can't make friends because there's no one here to make friends of. You're the lucky one. It's silly to pretend otherwise.'

Later, Laura softened towards Hugh, and would ask what he and Victor had been doing. Nothing very striking. Hopscotch by moonlight, follow-my-leader among the tombstones of the churchyard – and, of course, tree-climbing. The birds'-nesting of next year was planned; and Victor still boasted that he would get a heron's egg. Once, dared to it, Hugh had taken Victor on a complete tour of the outside of the Hall, pointing out particularly his own nursery window and also his father's study window. It glowed dimly in a large oblong, from the lamp on the other side of the heavy curtains. Sir Robert was working this evening. The boys backed away.

Even before Tom was back for the Christmas holidays, hunting started. Laura loved that; Hugh hated it. Then there were bonfires and potato-bakings out of doors; and indoors, in the schoolroom, Spanish chestnuts could be roasted. There was the Christmas party in the servants' hall for all the village children, their faces shiny with soap and water for the occasion, their eyes ravenously on Mrs Ashley's heaped jam sandwiches and cakes. In the past Victor had come with the others; this year he did not. He told Hugh that his father – Victor's – did not wish it.

The sensation of the end of the year was a motor-car – the first ever to pass through the park gates and down the avenue, at twenty miles an hour, to come to a standstill before the front entrance of Stanford Hall.

'Just supposing any of us had been on a horse,' Laura said indignantly. 'Coming at that rate and rattling and hooting!'

But she went gladly with the others when they had permission to view the novelty at close quarters. Permission was given by Lord Pinewood, the owner and enthusiast driver; and they also had to have their parents' approval of their presence at the front door at all. Only Sir Robert and Lady Hatton and their guests used the big front entrance of Stanford Hall; the children of the house, the servants, the tenants and others coming upon humbler business used the back door or a side door.

Lord Pinewood had come to consult with Sir Robert on important County affairs. He was an influence in the County, and Sir Robert – in Walter's words – cultivated his acquaintance like one o'clock. In Walter's opinion, Sir Robert had made up his mind to be somebody big, apart from having married the heiress of Stanford: 'He'll contrive to get himself chosen Member of Parliament here, or some such thing. And if he don't succeed in that – why, then he'll try for something big where he comes from, back in Yorkshire. You'll see.'

The conference in the study lasted nearly an hour; then Lord Pinewood left, making history again – not unexpectedly this time, naturally – by being the first person ever to leave the Hall by motor-car. Having watched the last puff of Pinewood exhaust-smoke, the children went into the house to get ready for their morning ride.

After Lord Pinewood's going, Sir Robert interviewed a tenant. Then he rang for Walter to tell Lady Hatton that he wished to see her in the study. 'And I thought I heard Master Hugh's voice on the other side of the baize door as you came in.'

'I hardly think so, Sir Robert. I fancy they have all gone

out riding, unless I am mistaken.' Walter closed the study door, then slipped quickly back through the baize door to the pantry: 'Hop it, you lot. He heard you all right.'

'Oooh!' said Margaret, and jumped wildly into the silver cupboard in her riding habit.

'Get out of there,' said Walter. 'Off with you all. Otherwise you'll be caught, and then it's me that will get into trouble. I'll get the sack.'

Sobered by this, the children tiptoed down the stone passage and out by the back door. Walter returned through the baize door, and found himself almost face to face with Sir Robert, standing attentively just outside his study.

'I thought I told you to go and find her ladyship.'

'Yes, Sir Robert. It occurred to me that she might be giving out the stores for the week to Mrs Ashley; but she must be in her boudoir.'

'Go the right way to the right place next time, and use your head properly as well as your feet.'

'Very good, sir.' To himself Walter said, 'Ratty. What's up? Trouble for her Ladyship, I'll be bound.'

Alone with his wife when she had joined him in the study, Sir Robert said: 'Pinewood certainly doesn't mind looking a fool, going gallivanting about the countryside in that vehicle of his.'

Lady Hatton agreed warmly: horseback was always more dignified; and more reliable too. She was surprised at Lord Pinewood.

'All the same, he's a shrewd man, and a very useful one,' said Sir Robert. But he had not summoned his wife to discuss motor-cars or Lord Pinewood's usefulness: his concern was with Hugh's future − 'I mean, the expenses of his going away to school.'

'Yes, Rob.'

He referred to a list in his hand. 'The items of clothing supposed necessary are absurd in number.'

'They are the minimum which the school asks for. As far as possible, Hugh is wearing Tom's cast-offs.'

'Of course.' But Sir Robert drummed martially with his fingertips on his desk, as he looked out of the window. The gravelly and childless view often soothed him; now it fortified him. 'We must not be stampeded into ridiculously unnecessary expense by these school authorities,' he said.

With a firm pencil he began to score out certain items on the list.

IO

Tom and Hugh sat opposite to each other in the train that was taking them away to boarding school. For Hugh this was the first time: the first time he had ever left home, ever been parted from his sisters, ever remembered a separation from Walter and the others, ever shut the nursery door behind him with such finality upon the rocking-horse, the white cat, the green parrot, the portrait of W. G. Grace . . .

Unfamiliar landscapes fleeted by outside the carriage window; they made Hugh's eyes ache. Eyelids and eyes were tired already with private tears.

There were other people in the third-class compartment, so the two boys could not talk freely. Occasionally Tom smiled at Hugh to encourage him. The first term at school would not be as bad for Hugh as it had been for Tom, because Tom would be there to protect his brother from the worst bullying. Hugh could rely on Tom.

When Hugh was not aware of it, Tom studied him anxiously. Until today Hugh had worn the clothes of a little boy: jerseys with kilt or shorts, and sailor suits for special occasions. Now, for the first time, he was dressed as a schoolboy in a knickerbocker suit – once Tom's – with Eton collar and tie. Above him on the rack lay his overcoat and bowler hat. This whole outfit had seemed to Hugh to brighten the gloomy January day a little: he felt himself at least looking like other boys of spirit and independence.

But Hugh's hair! Tom narrowed his eyes as he wondered how his father had allowed his mother to send Hugh off to school with those long curls. Hugh himself knew no better, and would be amazed and furious to be described as looking like a girl. Yet that was what they would say of him at school.

Tom clicked his tongue gently to himself and began to work out the brilliant beginnings of a campaign.

They had been put in charge of the guard, with strict instructions to do just what he told them when they had to change trains. Tom was experienced enough to know when they were coming into the station where this was to happen. He leant forward and said quietly to Hugh: 'We change here. Get ready, and the instant the train stops, follow me closely with your bag.'

So the guard found them gone, the other passengers had no idea where. Someone said, 'They seemed to know what they were about, anyway.'

Tom knew what they were about. He had locked the two of them inside one of the station lavatories. Then he said, 'We are not going to school –'

'Tom!' cried Hugh, in a joyful gratitude.

' – until we have had your hair cut.'

'Tom!' Hugh said again, differently; but Tom held up his hand as authoritatively as he could in the restricted space, and said, 'And don't utter a sound until I give the word. Otherwise we maybe overheard and caught.'

People came and went to the lavatories. Somebody came and called out in a general way, 'Anybody seen two boys who've lost themselves? Two boys, eh?' But nobody replied; and somebody went away.

For half an hour Tom and Hugh waited in their locked lavatory. Tom was the only one ever to speak, in lowest whisper, each time after consulting his watch. 'The train we came by is due to go now, but they're probably afraid we may still be on it. They'll be searching still.' Later, as a train whistled: 'There she goes! They've decided we can't be left on it after all; and, anyway, they can't wait any more.' A longer pause; then, eyeing his watch: 'Our connecting train should be coming in now. All the porters and everybody will be on the look-out, in case somehow we turn up to board it, after all ... But we don't.' Another train whistle:

'We don't; and it's off without us. We've missed our connection. The station people will be giving us up ... We'll allow them another ten minutes; then we'll escape.'

In due time and with the greatest caution they left their refuge. Tom reconnoitred the platform: 'All clear. Follow me – and look as if we're doing exactly what we always intended.' Without attempting the main exit, Tom led the way briskly along to the very end of the platform, where a small gate opened into the goods yard. 'I knew of this gate,' he said with satisfaction. They walked through the yard and on to the road without any question being asked by anyone.

Hugh was speechless, partly with admiration at Tom's cleverness and daring, partly from the continuing effect of the long silence imposed in the lavatory. But his face now shone with quiet hope.

They made their way into the town, passing a greengrocer's, where they stopped to buy apples and bananas. Eating these, they walked along until they found a barber's shop.

Hugh had hardly realized what Tom meant about his hair until the barber, scissors in hand, began to grieve for it: 'Beautiful, beautiful hair! How the ladies would envy such waves and curls! And so soft – and, if I may say so, of a most unusual dark chestnut colour. Very delicate. A shame – a crying shame to cut it; but I know what young gentlemen feel. No doubt long hair gets into the eyes when you're playing football and cricket ...' He sighed, and began to cut.

Tom paid the barber, and they left him. Then Hugh spoke: 'What do we do next, Tom?'

'I think we'd better go back to the station in the first place.' Tom was uneasily aware of having come to the end of his planning. He had worked out the brilliant beginnings of a campaign, and the beginnings were over, while the campaign was not.

'Shall we go on to school after all?'

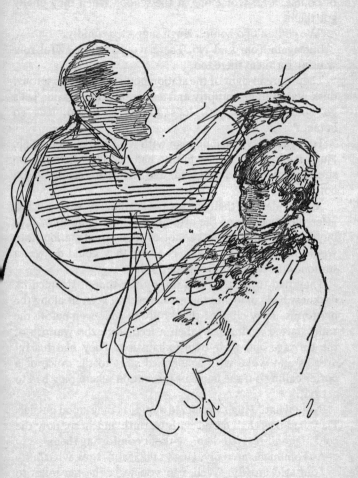

But Tom said No. As soon as they showed their tickets at the station, everybody would realize that here were the truants after all, and there would be a row at the station; and, of course, a far worse one at the school, when they finally got there.

'We couldn't go home?' Hugh suggested timidly.

But again Tom said No. There would be an awful row waiting for them there too.

They were in sight of the station now; the sun was setting; dusk was falling. Abruptly and desperately Hugh said: 'Let's go home. Please, Tom, let's go home. Please, let's go home. *Please.*'

Tom gave in. He had no plan with which to oppose Hugh. Hugh had no plan either, but he had his overwhelming desire to turn back to Stanford; and his desire carried them both.

A good deal of their term's pocket money was still left after the expenses of the afternoon. They spent all of it in buying two single tickets – not to their usual station; that would have cost too much. The best they could do was a station some ten miles from Stanford.

They had to wait for a train. By the time it steamed in, darkness had come and the gas-lamps had been lit along the platforms. They climbed thankfully in and, even before the train started again, had fallen asleep from the warmth of the carriage and their own exhaustion. They had fearful dreams and woke with a horrified start to the voice of a porter calling out the name of the station where they had to get out.

'Now what?' Hugh wondered aloud, as they stood outside. They had been half-dazed with warmth and sleep; now the cold night air revived them, without comforting them.

As Tom made no reply, Hugh said again, 'Now what?'

Tom said crossly, 'Well, can you walk the ten miles to Stanford, with your bag?'

'No.'

'Then we'll have to hire a cab.' There was one waiting; they got in and Tom told the driver where to go.

'Stanford Hall,' he said. 'Oh, yes. Sir Robert Hatton.'

The boys did not speak as they rattled and bumped along the lanes to Stanford. The cab stopped at the park gates, and the cabman was climbing down to open them. Tom said, 'We'll get out here. I'll pay you now.'

'That'll be ten shillings, sir.'

'Oh.' Hugh hauled the bags out, while Tom began to feel through his pockets; but they both knew it was useless. Tom said, 'I've only three shillings, I'm afraid.'

'Well, then, I'll take you down to the house and your father will pay.'

'No. Oh, no,' said Tom. 'Don't do that.'

But the cabman intended to have his full fare. He held the door of the cab open for them to get in again. The thought of their father's receiving the news of their unlooked-for return at the same time as a demand for ten shillings was too much for them – much too much for them.

'Come on, Hugh!' Tom said suddenly, and dived away, bag in hand, and with Hugh after him, through the little side gate and into the darkness ahead.

The cabman neither worried nor hurried; but he was determined. He shut up his empty cab, opened the gates and drove through and down the back drive towards the house. The boys, scudding ahead, could hear the cab-horse's slow hoof-beats behind them; looking back, they could see the advancing flicker of the oil lamps.

They reached the back door, slipped through it and – without hesitation under these circumstances – along the passage into the kitchen. Mrs Ashley was dishing up the servants' supper. When she saw the boys, she screamed and dropped a saucepan. Then she peered closely, picked the saucepan up again and said, 'My word, you didn't half give me a fright! I thought it was ghosts. Whatever's happened? Her Ladyship and Sir Robert will have a fit.'

'Where are they?' asked Tom.

'Still in the dining-room.'

'Could you get Walter quickly?'

But here was Walter now: 'Cor love a duck and strike me pink!' To him and to Mrs Ashley and to Elsie, who was now standing beside the other two with her mouth open, Tom explained briefly their plight. 'And so now what shall we do?' he asked. 'Hide in the attics, do you think; or in the sheds?'

'Well, now,' said Walter, 'they are bound to find out, you know.'

'There's the back door bell,' said Elsie, putting her mouth to normal use again with difficulty.

Tom groaned. 'That'll be the cabman for his ten shillings.'

'Well, now,' Walter said again, 'I haven't that amount. There's no getting round it: I'll have to ask Sir Robert for it. But at least I can spin a good tale about your missing your connexion, and the hair-cut, and the state you were in. And I'll say that Master Hugh don't look too grand, which is the truth. And now I'll tell you both something. A telegram has come from your headmaster saying you've not arrived as expected. So you see, your coming home will be more a pleasant relief than a surprise – at least, to her Ladyship.'

'But where shall we go?' Tom asked.

'Stay here. Sir Robert will never come along to the kitchen.'

So they stayed, and Mrs Ashley made them each an enormous jam-sandwich, and Hugh held his without eating it, as in a trance. Then Walter returned.

'It's all right,' he said. 'He didn't seem much upset – although, of course, he cut up rough over the ten shillings. But he said, that after what he'd heard, he supposed it might all have been far worse; and her Ladyship said I was to tell you both to go to bed at once and Elsie is to bring you each a

88

bowl of bread and milk, and she will come and say good night later.'

Hugh was too tired to say anything; he seemed to have been much too tired for a long, long time. The bag-laden escape from the cabman had been the last straw.

But Tom said earnestly, 'How can we ever thank you, Walter?'

'One day, perhaps. Now off to bed. And you too, Master Hugh.' He was looking at Hugh carefully for the first time. 'You're a proper boy and no mistake now, Master Hugh, with your hair cut. You're growing up quickly, that's certain.'

Hugh heard Walter's voice like the sound of a solemn bell in a dream. Later, upstairs, he was fast asleep when Elsie came with the bread and milk, and did not waken then or when his mother came.

To Tom, Lady Hatton said, 'Papa thinks that your actions were excusable under the circumstances which Walter described; but, of course, you will have to go back to school tomorrow. And Papa will not give you another five shillings each. You will get no more money this term, he says.'

She kissed him good night.

The next morning Laura and Margaret greeted the boys' return with amazement and delight Margaret did not trouble to understand Tom's explanations, but Laura listened attentively attentively, glancing often at Hugh.

After breakfast in the schoolroom they all went down to family prayers as usual, and afterwards heard the solemn confirmation of Sir Robert's judgement on the boys. He ended his speech: 'This must not happen again. I went bravely to school, in spite of disliking it – and worked very hard. Otherwise, where should I be now? Where you may end up, Hugh, if you do not apply yourself: breaking stones on the road.'

'Yes, Papa.'

'Now both of you go and get ready to leave again.'

Laura and Margaret went with them when they said their second good-byes to Walter.

'You'll see,' Walter said to Hugh, 'you won't mind going away this time nearly so much.'

'Why not?'

'It's just that the first time is much the worst; the other times won't matter.'

Hugh said: 'Laura wouldn't mind going even the first time.'

'People are different,' Walter said non-committally; and then added to Laura, 'Your time will come some day, Miss Laura.'

'That's the kind of thing Mrs Phillips says when she's trying to find us the very best fortunes in the tea-leaves,' said Laura.

'I know nothing of tea-leaves; but I know a lady of spirit when I sees her, Miss Laura, and I say your chance will come. And when it comes, you'll take it.'

Laura flushed. 'A lady of spirit' was so different – and so much better – than merely 'a lady'.

So the boys went back to school a day later than intended, and when they got there, things were not as bad as might have been expected. There were only reproaches, no real row; and nobody at school guessed what Hugh's hair had so recently looked like.

Another row developed. The headmaster wrote to Sir Robert Hatton to say that his younger son had not arrived with all the items of clothing necessary, and that the matron of the school had therefore bought him more. These, of course, would be charged to Sir Robert.

Sir Robert then wrote to Hugh saying that he wished he had never sent him to such an expensive school, and that he seemed to feel no gratitude. He had been disloyal to his parents. He could easily have insisted to the school authorities that the clothing he had come with was quite enough and that he could make do with it. Finally, Sir Robert said

90

that only half Hugh's pocket-money could be spent; the other half must be saved and put towards the expense of the unnecessary extras.

'He's forgotten that he docked our money altogether, anyway,' Tom said.

'And half nothing's nothing,' said Hugh. Secure in their poverty, they even laughed.

II

Was it that year or the next that Evie Tomlin died? Later, Stanford people could not quite remember: it was no unusual thing for a child to die, and Evie had been ailing for a long time.

It happened just before Tom and Hugh came home for their Easter holidays. Laura was the first to hear the news, by way of the back door. If you were intimate with all who came and went, you knew what had happened long before information reached the front of the house. The baker's cart called at the back door three times a week, with news as well as with bread. The postman's cart also called there. Even when the telegraph boy arrived with a telegram, it was common knowledge who had been taken ill or refused an invitation long before the message on the silver salver was opened by Sir Robert.

Laura was sorry; and the boys too, when they came home and were told; and Margaret – who was the same age as Evie – said, 'I wish I *had* had her as a friend.' But Evie had led such an indoor, invalid life that no one outside her own family had known her well.

Lady Hatton, on eventually hearing the news, said, 'Poor child!' But Lady Hatton, like her husband, had always had a thorough-going dislike of Evie's father as a schoolmaster. It was true that his duty was to educate, she said, but there was no need to go to absurd lengths. Simple reading, writing and sums, were enough for the Stanford village children, as for their fathers in *her* father's time. More would only make them dissatisfied with their lot. It was quite wrong of the schoolmaster to think of teaching them more.

Sir Robert said he had heard that the man's son (this was Victor) had ambitions to go to a university, and certainly he had airs above his station. There was not enough discipline these days. The whole situation was deplorable.

Then, on an afternoon not long after Evie's death, the Rector paid one of his usual visits to Sir Robert and Lady Hatton. Ernest, who served them with tea, carried his report back to the butler's pantry: 'Strike me, but there's a rare old battle on between the Rector and Sir Robert. All about repairs to the Rectory and the church; and then the Rector starts in on the school, and the schoolmaster comes into it all. Then Sir Robert goes up in flames – what a crying scandal it is, that man with his radical ideas, and should know his duties and when to keep his mouth shut, and teach respect for one's betters, and respect them himself, and –'

'And so on, and so on, and so on,' Walter interrupted snubbingly, since Ernest seemed about to over-reach himself in eloquence. 'And now Sir Robert's blown the Rector up, the Rector will likely go back and blow the schoolmaster up – if he'll stand for such a blowing up, since the child's death.'

Nobody knew exactly what happened next, because there were no outside witnesses of the interview between the Rector and the schoolmaster; but at the same time everyone knew that there had been an almighty row, one that would have beggared even Ernest's descriptive powers.

The Hatton children knew more than most because Victor and Hugh managed a meeting at the park fence. Victor, pale-faced and with a black armband, would only talk hurriedly and for the briefest time. He said that his father was going to leave Stanford at once, at all costs. He had come to Stanford only that Evie might have country air and country food; now that she was dead, nothing should hold him in such a place. He would take his family to London, where he could get as good a job, and where Victor would have a much better chance of scholarships.

Victor ended by saying that he would try to meet Hugh again at least once to say good-bye; but Hugh waited in vain

93

at the rendezvous on the next occasion. This coincided with Sir Robert and Lady Hatton's absence in Yorkshire for several days, and the children decided in a body to make one last attempt to get in touch with Victor. They went to the schoolmaster's house: all the blinds were drawn, and they found they had not the courage to knock on the front door. While they looked, the schoolmaster came out into the garden, saw them, and shouted furiously at them. They came away then.

'Victor's held prisoner until he goes,' Tom said, and they all looked sympathetically at Hugh, sorry for his loss. They gave Victor up, as though London had already swallowed him.

The next night the Stanford household went to bed as usual: the children in the nursery wing; all the servants, except Walter in the remote attics; Walter downstairs, next door to the silver cupboard. They went to bed and to sleep.

Laura, alert even in sleep, became aware of an unusual repetition of noise somewhere outside, but close. She woke herself properly and listened: a sharp, light, pattering noise, that ceased. She could not place it, but was sure it was wrong.

She got out of bed and went to the window: although there was a moon, there were also thick clouds on the move. She could see nothing.

The noise did not come again, but now she heard quiet footsteps somewhere in the house. Was there a burglar outside, and one already in? At that rate, she must wake Tom, and she could not go to do it while leaving Margaret alone and asleep. Rather against her better judgement she began to wake her, with a hand against Margaret's mouth to prevent a cry and her own mouth against Margaret's ear to give explanation and warning.

The footsteps were approaching – reached their door; the door began to open. Margaret, intent upon screaming, was tearing at Laura's hand, when the open door revealed Tom in his pyjamas.

'You're up,' he said.

'I heard something,' said Laura.

'I thought I did too,' said Tom. 'Something woke me.'

'Laura heard burglar's footsteps inside the house,' Margaret managed to get in; but Laura corrected her impatiently: 'No, no. Those were Tom's footsteps.'

'But how could Tom be woken by his own footsteps?' Margaret asked, very much muddled.

'Something just outside,' Laura said over her head, and Tom nodded.

Tom took charge. 'It's up to us to go and see. None of the servants would hear from their bedrooms up there, and there is no one else in our wing. It's our responsibility.'

'What about Walter?' After all, Walter was the appointed guardian of the silver and of the back door key. But Walter had gone to bed with a heavy cold and a hot toddy, and it would be inhumane or impossible to wake him.

So Tom went off to wake Hugh – who slept nearly as soundly as Margaret – and to get two pokers. He returned soon with all three.

'Now,' he said, 'we tour the inside of the house. Very quietly; then we're more likely to surprise anyone breaking in. If we do find burglars, Papa and Mama will be pleased with us: they've been expecting them for years. On the other hand, if there aren't any after all, we must avoid the awkwardness of anyone's finding out what we've been up to. So I say, we must go quietly and wake no one. You, Meg, will go in front, carrying the candle.' He gave it to her. 'Hugh next with his poker. Laura next –'

'With what weapon?' Laura asked briskly.

'Er – you'd better take the coal-shovel from the grate, as you're a bad shot, anyway. You'll have more chance of hitting the man on the head with that than with a poker. Then myself last, with the longest poker.'

'Do I have to go first?' Margaret asked.

'She is the smallest and the youngest,' Laura said, in her support.

'That's why the man or men will not be so likely to hit you,' said Tom. 'And then I'll have time to act. Besides, in file I can see over all of you. And I shall have the longest poker.'

Laura opened her mouth as if to make some further objection to the arrangements, but closed it again.

'I'm frightened,' said Margaret, shivering; and Hugh looked unhappy.

'There's nothing to be afraid of,' Tom said irritably. Hopeless of putting another point of view, Margaret did not contradict. With Margaret in the lead, the four got into line, all in their night-clothes and with bare feet.

It was possible to make a complete tour of the inside of Stanford Hall without once retracing one's steps; and this was what Tom proposed.

'Along our own passage, down the front stairs, past Papa's study and the small dining-room; then along the stone passage and into the great hall, across it, and up the old staircase into the old wing. Then through the panelling door half-way up the old stairs, and so up to the attics, and then back by the passage to the back stairs.

'As we go, we shall be able to hear if anyone is in the large dining-room or the drawing-room or the library.

'We must be very quiet as we pass the attic bedrooms, because of the servants. Mrs Ashley is always saying that she sleeps wretchedly.

'Rally to me at once if you hear any of the alarm bells ringing on windows or doors. The burglars will be trying to break in. I should not be surprised if the bell on the back door rang soon. They may be trying that door at this moment.'

Laura said: 'Why doesn't Jet bark? His kennel is just by the back door.'

'They've killed him, I expect,' Tom said. 'Now come on, all of you. You, Meg, mind that you open the doors very quietly with your right hand and carry the candle in the left. Don't go too quickly, or the candle will go out.'

They made their way like a panther seeking its prey, following Tom's route and going quietly and carefully. Thus they came to the great hall.

Margaret opened the door; the great space of the hall lay before them, and it was empty of other human life: so much they could see by candlelight and – more – by the moonlight now coming in over the tops of the shutters. But very ghostly in the moonlight stood the suits of armour and the noble marble busts; and the sidelong gaze of a score of painted Stanfords was fastened upon them in mysterious expectation. So very much was always expected of the children of the house . . .

They were standing still, awed by the sight. Then Margaret's nerve broke and she scuttled across the empty floor to the door at the other end, the others following her.

The candle-flame had flickered out as soon as Margaret began to run, but that did not matter. The children knew the house by the feel of its walls, the creaks of its floor boards, the smell of its stone and wood and tapestry. Within minutes they were up the old staircase, and had found the door concealed in the panelling and slipped through it. Then up to the attic floor where the servants slept, and on tiptoe past each door there; and on and on, until – here they were again at last, back at the girls' bedroom.

Tom was very pleased indeed. 'We woke no one, and you all behaved very well. Especially you, Meg, the youngest and smallest. But you shouldn't have let the candle go out.'

'I was frightened,' Margaret said doggedly.

'There was nothing to be frightened of. We've proved that now. No burglars after all.'

'All the same,' Laura said, 'I did hear something.'

Hugh looked anxiously at Tom, who said, 'Come on, Laura – admit we both imagined it.'

'No. It sounded – it sounded a little like hail.'

'There you are then: a freak hailstorm.'

'Only it sounded more as if things were being thrown, instead of falling.'

But for Tom the adventure had ended, and the mystery should have ended with it. He would have no further discussion, sent them all to bed and went himself.

Alone again in the nursery, Hugh's mind returned to an oddity of experience at the time of Tom's rousing him. They had not looked out of the nursery window, being anxious at once to rejoin Laura and Margaret; and Hugh had got straight out of bed and crossed immediately to the bedroom door. In walking over the floor on bare feet, he had been aware of treading on a slight scattering of some unpleasing, gritty substance. He had not mentioned this irrelevancy to Tom, had hardly paused upon it himself – but had remembered it.

Now he tested the floor again with his feet, and found the stuff – a little was near the middle of the room, but more was under the window; and suddenly he saw still more lying upon the window-sill, clear in the moonlight: gravel. It must be from the gravelled court outside, but how did it come to be here in his room? Certainly it had not been here before he went to bed. His window had been left healthily open at the top, and, noting it now, Hugh remembered Laura's description of the strange noise she heard: the light pattering sound that had a kind of *throw* to it. That was it: somebody had been throwing gravel up to his window to attract his attention.

Victor!

He was so sure of it that softly, quickly, he opened the window at the bottom and called Victor's name in a whisper – in no more than a whisper, because of the other three. He realized the truth of what Laura had once said: Victor was *his* friend.

There was no sign from Victor, and it seemed likely that he had gone away long ago, disappointed. But Hugh left his bedroom and, for the second time that night, went softly, quickly downstairs and to the back door. He knew where Walter kept the key – as Walter knew that they all knew. He took it and, having dismantled the alarm-bell, unlocked the door, opened it, and stepped out. In his kennel Jet lifted his head to look at him, then let it sink again, and followed his movements with undisturbed eyes.

Hugh searched for Victor or for some sign of Victor: there was nobody and nothing. He ended up by standing roughly where he thought Victor must have stood to throw the gravel, facing the nursery window, looking up towards it. He could hardly see it, because for the moment clouds covered the moon. Then they parted, and moonlight illuminated the window and the whole of that side of the house. His gaze travelled downwards from the window – directly downwards, drawn by awareness of something unusual at the bottom edge of his field of vision. On the ground immediately beneath his window, and leaning against the wall of the house, lay some kind of bundle or loosely-made parcel. It looked abandoned, like a parcel which a postman has left in despair of ever receiving an answer to his ringing and knocking.

Even before he found the label, Hugh knew the parcel must be for him. By the light of the moon he saw his own initials, H. H. The parcel seemed to have no weight other than that of its own newspaper wrappings, but he held it all the more carefully, tenderly.

He carried it indoors and upstairs, securing the back door behind him as before. In the nursery again, he lit a candle and began to unwrap layer after layer of the crumpled paper. The last layer revealed an egg, large and of a beautiful blue tinged with green; perfect. The heron's egg that Victor had always promised.

There was nothing to tell by what means Victor had at

last climbed the tree to the nest. He had blown the egg before wrapping it as a farewell present to Hugh.

Hugh showed the egg to the others the next morning. They exclaimed at its beauty and rarity; and Tom made Elsie come to see it; and they called on Walter to inquire after his cold and to show it to him, too.

That explained the burglars, Tom pointed out. He did not mind, because – whatever the reason – they had all done something decisive and brave last night. It was practice for the future, and that was the important thing.

But Hugh's mind dwelt on Victor. He realized sadly that they might never meet again; and, in fact, the Tomlins left Stanford for good on the day after the night of Victor's visit. The Hatton children learnt this later.

Often, afterwards, Hugh would recall Victor and wonder what exactly he was doing now. 'Making his way in the world,' Laura always said. Her mother would have said it contemptuously; but Laura spoke with respect.

12

So far Sir Robert Hatton's ambitions were unsatisfied. In the County he was still no more than the master-by-marriage of Stanford Hall. His wife would have thought that enough; he did not. Member of Parliament – Lord Lieutenant of the County – something like that was what he needed. For that you had not only to be the right person but to know the right people.

When Lady Hatton had been a girl and money had seemed to flow as easily and richly as the Teal itself, then huge and splendid parties of every kind had been held – luncheon parties, dinner parties, garden parties, and balls. One of Sir Robert's favourite economies was to entertain as seldom as possible. On the other hand, if you were really to know the right people, you had also to entertain them.

So there was to be a dinner party of the old-fashioned kind. The first the children knew of it was that Laura was to have a new dress – not Margaret as well, because clearly she would wear Laura's old one, as usual. The new dress was to be made as like the old one as possible of similar white material sprigged with forget-me-nots, and in identical style. Laura and Margaret had always been dressed alike. Laura ground her teeth at it.

Never before had they been required to appear on the evening of a dinner party. Tom now supposed that they were to dress up in order to be shown off to the guests in the dining-room beforehand; to curtsy or bow and say, 'How do you do?'

They confirmed with Walter that this was to be the arrangement. 'And don't you get in *our* way that evening,' Walter said sternly, 'because we shall be up to our eyes in it all. It's the big dining-room this time – twelve have accepted already; and Sir Robert's his usual self. So keep to the other side of the baize door; and whatever you do, don't upset Mrs Ashley. You know how violent she can get. It's all that standing over a hot kitchen range.'

The day of the dinner party arrived, with all the work of great and meticulous preparations by the staff; and by the evening, nerves were frayed. The even-tempered Walter ordered the children out of his pantry while he and Albert, the new footman, were touching up the silver and polishing the glasses. They sought out Elsie, who was just as busy, but excited and eager.

'Oh, I should like to see Miss Laura in her new dress, and the ladies! Perhaps I shall have a squint at them when they comes upstairs to leave their coats. And her Ladyship is to wear her tiara, isn't she? And all her jewels. And Sir Robert his pink evening tails.'

Tom said, 'Thank goodness we don't have to dress up anything like that.'

'But I like you in your Eton suit,' said Elsie. 'You look a proper little gent.'

'It's bad enough to have to wear Eton suits on a Sunday,' said Hugh. 'Those white stiff collars make your neck sore.'

'That's the price of being a gentleman,' Elsie said reverently.

'Well, then, I wish we weren't.'

'And I wish I weren't a lady,' said Laura. 'I hate wearing silly, frilly dresses with bows and sashes and all the rest. I'd rather wear stiff collars.'

'Oh, you would look funny!' Elsie was giggling, but, seeing Laura's expression she stopped: 'You would have made a good boy, Miss Laura.'

Laura was the one who dreaded most what had to be faced that evening; Tom cared the least. When the time came, he dressed quickly in his Eton suit and went along to his sister's room. He found Laura lying on her bed in floods of tears; she was only partly dressed in the new white frock.

'What's the matter?'

She got up then, rage replacing despair. 'Look – just look at this awful thing I'm supposed to wear! I look like – like a white plum pudding. I look like a baby – why should I be dressed exactly like Meg, who is years and years younger? I can't and won't wear it. I can't. I won't.'

Tom said calmly, 'Then don't.'

'What? But I'll get into awful trouble.'

'You have to start somewhere. *We* have to start somewhere.'

'You are right.' She began to take the dress off, pulling and tugging at it viciously, hoping to tear it. 'I'll wear my old blue serge dress instead.'

'I'd like to do the same, said Margaret, making as if to take off the white party dress she had just put on.

'No, don't,' Tom said. 'You look all right, and it isn't fair to bring you into this. Laura is much older – nearly grown up.'

At that moment Hugh walked in, wearing only his underclothes: 'What's up?'

Tom, in charge of Laura's case, explained; and Hugh said, 'I'm glad. Let's make a stand. I haven't dressed properly because, when I put on my trousers, they wouldn't meet. So I'll come down to the party like this; and you, Laura, come down as you are now and give the guests a treat. Let's shame Mama and Papa!'

They all laughed hysterically, particularly Laura, who threw her discarded dress on the floor and jumped upon it repeatedly, the others encouraging her. They were too excited to observe the figure of Hortense appearing in the doorway. She had been sent by Lady Hatton to see whether the children were nearly ready to go down to the drawing-room. She stood in silence, saw, and went back at once to report the rebellious scene to her mistress.

So Lady Hatton appeared among them, awe-inspiring in her long black lace dress, arms bare and jewels sparkling in the fading light. A chill silence fell upon her four children.

'Why are you not dressed, Laura?' their mother said in a harsh voice. 'Or you, Hugh? Get ready immediately, or I shall send for Papa.

Laura stood her ground in her underclothes, her legs apart, her arms folded: 'I'm not going to wear that horrible frock. I'm not going to be made a laughing-stock!'

'You ungrateful child! When I got Papa to buy that lovely material, and Hortense has taken so much trouble to make it up for you!' She turned to Tom as to the eldest, the heir to Stanford, her hope. 'Tom, you must tell Laura to get ready.'

Tom was very pale. He knew the other three were watching him, waiting for him to speak. In the past they had always relied upon him, but often – although they would never admit it – he had let them down. Laura was remembering those occasions as she watched him: he could see it in her eyes . . .

'Tom, tell Laura to get ready.'

'No, Mama, I am not going to. Laura looks silly in the dress, as she says; and Hugh can't get his trousers on because they've grown too small.'

Lady Hatton was staggered. 'Such impudence! I shall tell Papa.' She tried to regain control of the situation. 'Your dress is very suitable, Laura; and you must put it on at once.' Laura did not stir, and Lady Hatton turned to Hugh: 'You never told me your trousers were too small. They were perfectly all right last term.'

'No, they were not,' Hugh said. 'Matron wrote to you about them and said I must have a new suit, and I had a letter from Papa saying you had decided it was quite unnecessary.'

Their mother did not deny this; she only said, 'Well, then, Hugh, you must wear Tom's last sailor suit; you will not have grown too big for that.'

Hugh was about to say, 'I'm not going to,' when Tom began steadily to speak: 'You bring this kind of misery on us, Mama, because Papa is too mean – and you seem to agree with him – to buy us any new clothes. That's not all. We don't get enough to eat. And that's not all. We are kept short of all kinds of things, just so that Papa can keep all the horses he wants and you can live at Stanford Park like Grandfather.'

'It's wicked – wicked of you to speak so of your father and mother, Tom, who have brought you up in this lovely place, with special governesses, and schools, and wholesome food! It's very bad for children to eat rich food; and Papa says you must learn not to waste money. And, anyway, Papa keeps the ponies for you to ride.'

'I don't want a pony,' Hugh said. 'I'd rather have clothes that fit and boots that don't let in the water.'

'And now that I'm nearly grown up,' Laura said, 'I want to be able to live my life as I choose. I don't want just to be a lady – even a beautiful lady, like you. You dislike me because of that. And Papa dislikes me, too, and despises Meg. He makes fun of Meg sometimes, and it's not fair. She can't help being as she is.'

Lady Hatton struggled to speak, and failed. She had never dreamt that her children could rise against her like this, with a voice for all the grievances of childhood. At last she managed to say, 'I am ashamed of such guttersnipe behaviour. Papa and I thought it would be a great treat for you to come down and see the dining-room and all the guests. I certainly shan't arrange it another time. You will all now go to bed, and I shall not have any of the fruit salad sent up, as I had intended. And Papa will speak to you in the morning.' She gathered up her train in one hand and swept from the room.

A silence fell upon the four children until their mother's footsteps had died away. Then Laura said, 'I'm so afraid that now Papa will try to separate us in the holidays.'

Hugh said, 'What shall we do?' and Margaret looked like crying.

They turned to Tom, who had been braver than any of them had dared to hope. He said slowly, 'I couldn't help thinking that Mama really agreed with a good deal of what we said. Walter has often said that she and Papa have rows and it's nearly always about money. About his meanness. That includes his meanness to us.'

They considered Tom's theory; and Laura said, 'It's possible. I must say I thought that if Mama hadn't been so furious, she would have been crying. She was really upset.'

Support for Tom's theory came most unexpectedly with the reappearance of Hortense to deliver a message from their mother: 'You may all go down to see the dining-room laid with the gold plate and to watch the guests go in; but you are not to come into the drawing-room, for it is too late. You must, of course, dress properly. You must hurry. They go to dinner in five minutes.' Hortense could not resist adding, 'This is kind of your mother, when you have been *si méchants.*'

It was evident that their mother had relented towards them. Laura was of the opinion that she would not tell Papa at all. For themselves, since they no longer needed to go into the drawing-room where the guests were gathering, it did not matter what clothes they wore. Laura was willing to put on her crumpled new dress; Hugh wore Tom's old sailor suit.

They walked quietly down the front stairs and entered the state dining-room by the entrance used for bringing in the dishes. There was no one in the room; and its splendour overwhelmed them. The shutters of the tall windows had been closed on the night, and the many candles of the candelabra had been lit. By the candlelight they saw the famous gold plate laid out on the damask table-cloth, the gilt dishes filled with grapes, peaches and pineapples, the smaller silver dishes filled with nuts and chocolates, the great silver centre-piece of the three goddesses. Flowers and asparagus fern made the table a fairyland.

Margaret broke their spellbound silence by whispering, 'Let's each take one chocolate.'

They agreed to take one from each of the four dishes – no more, or Walter would get into trouble. Ceremoniously they walked round the table, each making his or her choice. 'Mine has a violet,' said Margaret.

'Hush!' said Tom. 'I can hear them coming. Quick!'

They ran out the same way as they had entered and quietly opened the door leading into the great hall. From here, without being seen, they could watch the procession from the drawing-room through the hall to the dining-room.

'Here they come,' said Tom.

'Don't they look funny!' Margaret said. 'Walking arm-in-arm in twos, like dogs tied together.'

'They're always like that.'

'Look at Mama with Lord Pinewood! She's smiling at him like anything. You'd never think she'd been in a fury.'

'And Papa is making up to Lady Pinewood.'

'For what he can get out of her, I should think. They're Liberals, Walter said, and Papa is a Liberal too.'

'He might be more liberal with us.' This was Laura.

They commented in whispers upon each couple that passed into the dining-room. Then Albert had shut the door upon the last of them, and there was nothing more to see.

They went through the baize door then and took up their usual position near the back stairs. From here they were able to intercept Albert on his way to and from the dining-room with the dishes. He gave them some account of the diners' conversation and, from the remains of the fish course, half a piece of fried sole each. Eating this, they retired up the back stairs to their bedrooms and eventually to sleep.

The whole occasion had passed off a great deal better than the children could have hoped. Much later that night, Sir

Robert also reflected with satisfaction upon the party just over: 'One can say it was a success, Linda. I told Pinewood that I hoped to stand as a Liberal candidate at the next General Election, and he was most encouraging. Most encouraging. Said he was glad some men of my age and ability wanted to serve their country. His actual words were "with your brains and energy". But he seemed disappointed the children did not come in; said Laura was grown very pretty, wasn't she? He has a son some six years older.'

'You mean that he has his eye on her for the son?' said Lady Hatton. 'I think so too. But, of course, he is a jumped-up man; not one of us. His father made his way in the world.'

'You forget that my father also made his way in the world.'

Lady Hatton was silent. In fact, she could never forget.

'Anyway, such things don't matter these days; and the Pinewoods could be very useful to me in politics. But why didn't the children come into the drawing-room before dinner? They would, for once, have been an asset; and I thought it had all been arranged.'

Lady Hatton drew herself up. 'I was ashamed of their clothes, and I thought it might reflect upon you.'

Sir Robert tutted. 'Perhaps now you see why I told you the other day that it's essential to sell some of the Stanford possessions in order to have more ready money. If you had not been so obstinate in refusing my advice, then you might have had the cash to buy the children what was necessary – if it *was* necessary. I hope this will be a lesson to you.'

This ended the conversation and they began to go to bed.

13

NOWADAYS Laura was sometimes afraid of Stanford. It seemed to her like a net – the silk net of a dead conspiracy. Look at the result of their stand on the memorable evening of the dinner-party: apparently nothing of importance. Their mother never afterwards referred to it, and clearly she had allowed no word of their revolt to reach their father. Yet on that occasion they had at last asserted themselves and each one of them – always excepting Margaret – felt different afterwards. They could never feel quite the same again; they had changed in themselves.

Their mother's attempt to make them wear clothes too young for them – to dress Laura like Margaret – had been part of the conspiracy. She did not want them to grow out of childhood and be less manageable. She was against change.

Stanford itself, her accomplice in the conspiracy, seemed to change only by stealth. In the park the lime trees grew a hundredth of an inch in girth; the oak tree one-eighth; nobody marked their growth. Inside the house chintzes faded only slowly; stair-carpets aged with imperceptible wear. The clocks ticked and people came and went, mostly the same people in the same clothes. Ernest had left for another post; but his place and his uniform had been taken over by Albert. Elsie had wished to leave at the same time as Ernest, but the offer of a rise of six pounds a year decided her to stay; and in time she succeeded Mrs Ashley as cook. Walter Mark was still there; Alice, the head housemaid, was still there; William Kemble, Dan Power, Phillips – they were all there, down to the odd man who went through the refuse bin. At least, he had died, but he had been replaced by another odd man so like him in general appearance and manner that people forgot that there had been a change.

If nothing else had been allowed to tell them, the children knew they were growing up because of the childhood memories that seemed to be accumulating behind them. When they were together, they quite often began sentences with, 'Do you remember . . .?'

Tom, who was now in his last year at school, preparing for Sandhurst, said, 'Do you remember our tree-house?' Together they had wandered out on to the lawns, until they stood beneath the cedar of Lebanon. 'Here's the rope we used, still sound. You hated having to get up by that rope, Meg.'

'Yes. I was so afraid of falling.'

They were all looking upwards to dizzying height upon height of branch. Laura supposed that it had been dangerous; and Hugh agreed – 'But then we were in practice.'

'Nonsense!' Tom said, unable to resist the unintended challenge. With the aid of the rope he flung himself on to the first branch, and then started to climb. He climbed to the level where they had made their platform and had sketched walls round it – all now much decayed. He did not stop here, but went on climbing, while the other three craned their necks to watch him. He reached the top of the sixty-foot tree. There he sat on the topmost branch, waving his left hand, holding on firmly with his right.

'Come down!' Margaret begged fearfully; and while she was in the middle of saying it, there was a sharp crack and the branch on which Tom sat – not one of the stoutest branches – broke. They saw it happen, and saw Tom, with brilliant agility, manage to drop on to the branch below and continue the descent as though he had always intended it thus.

But this pretence broke down when he reached the ground and saw the white faces of Laura and Hugh, and Margaret's pouring tears. 'I didn't mean to do that,' he said. 'I'm sorry, Meg.'

For answer, she hugged him; and Laura said, 'You might have been killed.'

'You might, you know,' said Hugh.

'I can't think why that branch broke,' Tom said. 'In the old days, when we were little, we climbed right up there often and often.'

Hugh said, 'You're twice as heavy now as then.'

'And perhaps that particular branch has grown weaker with age and wind and weather,' Laura said. 'Although, of course, it doesn't look any different.' That was part of the Stanford conspiracy.

This happened in the short Easter holidays of the year 1914: the year when Tom was due to leave school for Sandhurst and the army; the year when Hugh – who had out-run Tom in leaving school – passed from the Naval College at Osborne to become a naval cadet at Dartmouth. This was also the year when Laura would have finished with the schoolroom and Fräulein Schmidt for good. She could have enjoyed the prospect more if she had seen any worthy occupation to take its place. Walter had once promised her she would have her chance; but there was no sign of it yet.

Laura and Margaret saw Fräulein Schmidt off in the dog-cart to the station on the day that Tom and Hugh were due back in the afternoon for the summer holidays.

As they watched the dog-cart disappear, Margaret said gloomily, 'Mama says she'll be back from Germany in September, and then I'll have lessons all alone with her, without you.'

'She may not come back. Walter thinks there may be a war with Germany. If things go on, he says.'

'Really?' Margaret brightened, and her mind turned more blithely to the afternoon. At that moment Dan Power appeared from the woodyard and greeted them with a smile, a touching of the cap, and a 'Nice morning, miss,' to each.

'Oh, Dan,' Margaret cried, 'you'll be seeing us in the early mornings again, now that Tom and Hugh are coming home.

We could get eggs down the river again. Do you know of nests?'

'I know of some, miss, of course; but I think the young gentlemen would rather go a-shooting nowadays. Sir Robert says I am to take them out ferreting and shooting vermin.' He laughed and stamped his feet, a sign that he was pleased. 'I says to Sir Robert that Master Tom could use my twelve-bore gun now, and Master Hugh go from the rook rifle to the sixteen-bore single barrel; and he says, "Yes, Dan, but don't let 'em waste cartridges".'

'I don't care for shooting,' Margaret said, disappointed. 'I don't like the bangs and dead things.'

Dan said cheerfully, 'We has to keep the vermin down, miss,' and stamped away with his gun under his arm and his black retriever at his heels.

When he had gone, Laura said to Margaret: 'I've told you, Meg: Tom and Hugh are very grown up nowadays. They won't want to do baby things like exploring down the river. I want to get them to come out riding, because soon the cub-hunting will start and William says we must get the ponies fit.'

'Oh!' Then, pleadingly, 'But don't you remember, Laura, when we raided the kitchen garden and feasted on apricots and peaches? Tom led us then. He'd still like to do that again, surely?'

'No,' Laura said, closing the conversation.

That afternoon they settled in the nursery to watch for the historic event of Tom and Hugh returning together by motor-car from the railway station. This car was a fairly recent innovation of Sir Robert's. The railway strike of 1911 had alarmed him: he feared that it might happen again some day, and then he might miss an important political meeting. So he had at last bought a car. At first, he had not allowed any of the children to ride in it.

At the beginning of the holidays, the girls had always listened from the nursery window for the sound of the brougham, dog-cart or horse-bus rattling down the drive. On a still day it could be heard four hundred yards away, with the climax as the horse went under the stable archway like a clap of thunder. With a car, however, the rubber tyres deadened nearly all the noise.

'Hark!' said Laura. 'Isn't that something now?' And a few seconds later William Kemble, at the wheel of the car, sounded his horn and drove smartly from under the archway.

The car stopped, and there was Hugh, in his naval uniform, getting out, and then Tom, grown as tall as William himself. At the sight of them, Margaret was all for flying down to the back door to greet them. Laura held her back: 'I'm not sure they won't see Mama and Papa first: and it would spoil our meeting if we got mixed up with all of them. We'll wait at the top of the back stairs.'

They waited without impatience, now that the reunion was so near. When Tom and Hugh appeared, they kissed and embraced each other, laughing for joy; and then, as soon as possible, they set off together on a round of visits to old friends – Walter and Elsie and Dan Power and the rest – and to old haunts. By the park gates they wished, as they had always done.

That evening they were crossing the stable yard from an hour of fishing. They heard the dressing-gong – a signal for the three elder ones to change for dinner. Walter, knowing they were out, had opened the baize door so that they could hear the warning clearly.

They hurried to change, and then met again in the schoolroom to watch Margaret eating her bread and milk.

'I wish that I were you, Meg,' said Laura. 'This is much nicer than eating with Mama and Papa and being told to sit up; or "Where are your manners – " or "Ladies don't behave like that".'

'But you have chicken and fruit and cream,' said Margaret.

'It's not worth it.'

'Especially at the beginning of the holidays,' Hugh said. 'Then Papa always goes on to Tom and me about extravagances, and how did we spend all that money last term.'

'Unless you can get him into a good mood,' Tom said. 'The thing to say is something like, "Someone said what a good landlord you are"; or, "No one can ride Firefly like you".'

'You must say who said it,' Laura said. 'I always quote William. He likes that.'

The second gong went, and the three filed out of the schoolroom, down the passage, through the door to the front stairs, and so down to the smaller dining-room and their parents.

During dinner the conversation was mostly about local politics, the gentry, and economy; and it was conducted by Sir Robert. Occasionally Lady Hatton would have a chance to change the conversation with some brief remark, such as, 'Rob, poor Mrs Barnes is very ill. Laura, remind me tomorrow to send her some soup'; or, 'Power told me the partridges are going to be very good this year.' The three young people remained silent as far as possible.

When dinner had ended, Lady Hatton and Laura left the dining room, and Walter poured Sir Robert a glass of port. Tom and Hugh were given half a glass each. Then Walter and Albert left the dining room.

The door shut, Sir Robert said, 'Now sip slowly,' and went on talking about his problems. The small dose of port, meanwhile, began to glow in Hugh and gave him courage. When there was a pause, he said, 'Papa, do you think there is going to be a war with Germany?'

Sir Robert looked at Hugh in surprise and said, 'A very good question, my boy.' Hugh felt his blood rising in a blush, but his father did not notice it. Sir Robert's remark had been partly to give himself time to answer Hugh's question, by referring privately to another very good question: Did he, Sir Robert, want a war?

He looked at the ceiling and took a sip of port. 'Yes,' he said, 'I think there may be a war, but not if the Government really count the cost. If there is, it may ruin my chance of standing for Parliament at the next election.' He frowned: the realizing of his political ambitions had been so very long delayed. 'And if war is declared, we should almost certainly have to leave Stanford. It would be impracticable to stay on here.' Now he nearly smiled, and suppressed the near-smile instantly. It would be his great chance to get free of Stanford, that ancient white elephant.

Hugh said: 'Anyway, if there is a war, our navy is better than all the other navies put together.'

Tom said: 'I don't think there will be a war.' His tone was regretful. After all, he wanted to be a soldier.

Later that evening, upstairs again with their sisters, the two boys returned to the subject, and Laura observed, 'Mama says that the King being related to the Kaiser, there won't be a war.'

'I'm not sure it would make all that difference,' Hugh said doubtfully.

'If there is a war,' said Laura, 'I shall go and tend the wounded.' The idea had suddenly come into her head; it was going to remain there.

'Oh, you mean join the Red Cross,' Tom said. 'Good idea, Laura. I've always thought some of the ladies must have a very nice time entertaining the officers.'

'No!' Laura spoke so violently that Tom was taken aback. 'No, I should train as a proper nurse; I shouldn't just be a lady playing at it.' Suddenly she saw that, if war came, this might be her chance, and she must take it.

Margaret had specially stayed awake to enjoy their company, and now begged: 'Do let's talk about something nice. Not war.'

'All right,' Tom said. 'Something that Meg wants to talk about.'

'The things we used to do,' Margaret said eagerly .'Do you remember . . . ?'

So once again they played this new game of 'Do you remember?'

14

ON the morning of 5 August Laura and Hugh woke early.

Laura lay quite still except for her head, which she turned slowly from one side to the other on the pillow as she looked round the bedroom. She had slept here ever since leaving the nursery, as a little girl, and nothing had ever changed. The wallpaper, the carpet, the curtains, the furniture – all were the same. Over the years there had been a few additions, such as Margaret's bed and Margaret herself. For most of her life she had shared a bedroom with Margaret.

On the dressing-table lay the ebony-backed hand-mirror which Laura had been given when she was younger; it was years ago that she had cracked the glass and it had remained cracked ever since. Her eyes rested on the mirror, then closed tightly; her whole face became still. She willed herself to go sleep again, and – as with most of the not-impossible things that Laura set her mind to – she achieved this.

When Hugh woke, he looked about him with an habitual satisfaction – although at the back of his mind lay some foreboding that he could not quite put a name to. All the familiar things of the nursery reassured him: the rocking-horse, the white cat, the green parrot, the little girl like poor Evie Tomlin (what was Victor doing now?), the bearded cricketer. He had seen them all thousands of times before. He had gone away from them to school, and come back; and to Osborne, and come back; and now to Dartmouth. Not long ago he had thought he would hate going into the Navy, because his parents had always planned it for him. But then he had begun to see that a naval career would mean freedom for him even earlier than for Tom: at sixteen he could be sailing the high seas as a midshipman. In no time right round the world; and then, of course, back here again.

But now the foreboding at the back of his mind came forward and declared itself: of course, the garden party next week. They would all have to dress up – Laura rather more suitably than in the past; this was her victory over her mother. He and Tom would have to wear white flannels, in case they were needed to make up a set at tennis.

Bad luck! And then in September there was to be a shoot, but Hugh knew that he would not be considered old enough to take part. Old enough for a garden party; too young for a shoot. Bad luck indeed.

To cheer himself he decided to visit Walter downstairs. The papers would have come, and they could read the cricket news together. He decided not to wake the others, he would have Walter to himself.

He tiptoed along the passage and down the back stairs as so often before, and then to the butler's pantry. He came so quietly that he surprised Walter, who was engrossed in reading a newspaper which he had already ironed out for Sir Robert.

'Hello,' said Hugh. 'Cricket?'

Walter had started. 'No. Look at this.'

In thick black type: *WAR DECLARED.* Hugh saw it, and felt himself go cold, breathless, dizzy. He sat down in a chair. He felt that the end of the world had come.

Then he leaned across to grip Walter by the arm. 'What about Papa?'

'He doesn't know yet. I haven't called him. I was going in about ten minutes with his can of hot water.'

'No,' said Hugh. 'I'll go and wake the other three and we'll break the news.'

Walter coughed and scratched his head. 'I think I'd better call him first.'

'No,' said Hugh. 'It's for us.'

'What about our cricket?'

'No,' Hugh said scornfully – the first time he had ever scorned cricket. And, 'I'm going now.'

He roused Tom, Laura, and Margaret with his news; and they instantly saw that they must be the ones to tell their parents.

Tom said: 'Perhaps Papa will rejoin his old Yeomanry regiment in Yorkshire.'

'Really? Really?' cried Margaret. She saw Stanford without her father, and the prospect was like an endless summer day.

Hugh shook his head doubtfully. 'He always says his work on the County Council is very important. And then there are the Territorials, too. And I don't think he'd ever leave Mama alone here at Stanford: he'd be afraid of her having a good time and entertaining her old friends.'

'But he loves Yorkshire; and he hates it here.'

'I think what may decide him,' Laura said, 'is that he was only a Second Lieutenant in the Yeomanry. He would hate being under anyone.'

Talking in whispers, they had reached the door of their parents' bedroom. 'You knock,' Tom said to Laura. She did so, and they heard their mother say, 'Come in, Hortense.'

They went in and at once began, each in turn, to kiss first their father and then their mother, saying, 'Good morning, Papa and Mama.' Sir Robert had started bolt upright in the four-poster bed at their entry, and was demanding, 'What's the meaning of this? And why have we not been called?' He reached up and pulled the long red bell-cord, and far, far away a bell sounded for Walter. 'And what's the time?'

'About seven,' said Laura. Her eyes were brilliant, and none of the others questioned her leadership now. 'And we thought you would like to know that war has been declared.'

Sir Robert did not speak, but pulled the cord again more violently. Meanwhile, Lady Hatton had drawn the two girls to her on the other side of the big bed to embrace them, saying, 'How dreadful! What shall we all do without Papa?'

At that Sir Robert jumped out of bed and stood quivering in his nightshirt, feet bare.

'Will you be called up to your old regiment?' Laura asked.

'No!' His eyes flashed at the assembled company. 'What a ridiculous suggestion! My services are essential here – *here*!'

Almost at the same moment there was a knock on the door leading into Sir Robert's dressing-room – this must be Walter – and another on the door through which the children had come. Through this door a white-faced Hortense now entered; she eyed the scene, put down the can of hot water for her mistress, pulled the curtains violently back and then walked out, slamming the door behind her. Hortense had heard the news: France was in danger. She was feeling particularly French.

Meanwhile, through the other door, Sir Robert was giving Walter a number of orders – the time for breakfast, with prayers afterwards – 'all will attend'; and William Kemble to have the motor-car by the front door by eleven o'clock. Sir Robert must go to the Town Hall in Honeford.

'Very good, Sir Robert,' the voice of Walter said, over and over again.

When he had gone, Lady Hatton said, 'You are quite right, dear. We must not panic, but show an example to the servants. All must go on as before. Now, run along, children, and have your breakfast in the schoolroom as usual.'

It almost seemed as if things could really go on as before. True, Hortense packed her trunk and gave her notice and set off back to France that very day, and of course her departure made a difference. How would Mama manage without a lady's maid? How could she do her hair? How could she dress herself? Laura and Margaret would also be without Hortense's services; but they were heartily glad of it. It was arranged that Alice, the head housemaid, should help out.

The garden party was not cancelled, and when the day came it seemed as if little had changed. No one besides Hortense had left or joined up, even from the village. The weather was fine, sunny and cloudless. Only the war news was dark.

By the mid-morning of the day of the garden party Elsie had made all the cakes, the fruit salad laced with brandy, the still lemonade. Meanwhile, the tennis and croquet lawns had been marked and the chairs put out. But later that morning Laura observed in the stable yard a pony and trap which she had not seen before. She went out inquisitively, and was met by one of the under-grooms. 'A man has come to take all our horses for the army,' he said breathlessly. 'A Remount Officer. Mr Kemble says Sir Robert must be told at once. Mr Kemble told the man that he could not look round before Sir Robert came, but he says, "I'll look round first and see him afterwards".'

Laura turned and ran straight back into her father's study. He snapped, 'Don't burst in like that, Laura. Go back and knock at the door.'

'It's too urgent,' Laura said, and told him of the Remount Officer. Sir Robert jumped up and left the room, ringing the bell as he went, so that, before he reached the baize door, Walter had appeared.

'My hat and riding whip.'

'Very good, Sir Robert.' Hat and whip were handed from the hall slab as Sir Robert passed on his way to the stable yard.

Laura told Walter what had happened. 'Perhaps he's gone to give the Army a hiding,' Walter suggested humorously.

'I hope he does,' Laura said seriously. 'Never heard such cheek – taking people's horses!'

Walter looked at her thoughtfully. He was thinking that occasionally she was very like her father – and how angry she would have been to know it! He was also thinking that, with the war news what it was, there was little wonder that the Army was commandeering the horses it badly needed. All he said was, 'Ah.'

In the end Sir Robert had to let the horses go. Four were chosen, and Laura cried when she heard their names: Minstrel, Black Bess, Morningside and Kingsway. 'The two best hunters and carriage horses!' she wept. They were to go as officers' chargers and as gunner horses. William Kemble was almost in tears, too.

So the day of the garden party had started badly; and in the afternoon only half the expected number of carriages arrived, few drawn by more than one horse. There was, however, a Rolls-Royce, and in it Lord and Lady Pinewood and their son, an officer in the Grenadier Guards. Sir Robert had particularly hoped for their coming.

For most of the afternoon Margaret fielded balls hit off the lawns. Tom and Hugh played two sets of tennis; and Laura partnered John Pinewood in a game of croquet. After this game, he said, 'I've never seen your North Garden,' and Laura said, 'I'll show it to you.'

They wandered off through a maze of shrubs and yew hedges. The walk was silent until John Pinewood asked: 'What's that, Miss Hatton?'

'A trench that we dug ourselves.'

'How deep it is!'

'Deep enough for us to hide in,' Laura said. She warmed a little to this story. 'We used to boil moorhens' eggs here, and do things like that.' He had smiled, and she went on. 'We used to come here often in the very early morning, or when Mama and Papa were away.'

'Why then?'

'We might have got into trouble.'

'But what for?'

On the spur of the moment, without directly answering him, Laura said: 'They've always wanted me to grow up to be a lady and marry whom they want and not whom I want. I don't want to marry – at least, not for a long time –

not till I've *done* something.' As she spoke she looked at John Pinewood and their eyes met. Hers were defiant, but he smiled again, and said, 'Miss Hatton, you are very beautiful. You could marry whom you wish.' He had put out his hand to grasp hers, but she quickly put both her hands behind her back. He turned in order to pretend that he had not noticed it, and they began to walk back the way they had come.

Laura softened, let her hands appear in front of her, and said, 'When do you go to France?'

'Any day now. I'm on forty-eight hours' leave, and I've come home to say good-bye to Mother and Father. Mother tells me you may be coming to nurse in our house – it's being turned into a convalescent home for officers, you know. My mother and yours are both very keen on the Red Cross, of course.'

'I don't want to be a Red Cross nurse in an officers' convalescent home,' Laura said.

Tom and Hugh were coming towards them. Tom called out joyfully, 'Your father's been talking to me, John. Says the war may be over in a few months. Says he can get me a commission at once, without my going to Sandhurst. Otherwise I may miss the fighting.'

'It would certainly save a lot of time and sweat,' John said. 'And you could always stay on after the war.'

Tom's face glowed as they all walked back together to the lawns. These were now almost deserted; the party was over. The guests were saying good-bye to Sir Robert and Lady Hatton in front of the house, and making ready to mount into their traps or broughams. Their names were being called by Walter in his deep, powerful, respectful voice; in the background William Kemble was organizing the approach of the carriages one by one to the front door.

The last carriage left; the park gates were shut. A great silence wrapped Stanford Hall again; the whole place seemed to sink into sleep, as the sun went down. Even the cooing of pigeons and the occasional notes of other birds had ceased. Only the gentle sound of the river continued. It was difficult to believe that the world outside this world was not also at peace.

But in September Hugh was allowed to take part in the shoot, after all – the first time he had shot partridges in the company of other grown-up guns and with beaters. The reason was that most of those who were asked had refused.

In the early morning of that day, there was a thick haze, but by half past ten the sun had pierced it. The weather promised to be warm. Dan said, 'Walk steadily, keep your eyes open, and don't fire too quickly; for them partridges will sit light on the turnips on a hot day.'

By lunch-time the bag was fourteen brace of partridge – of which Hugh had shot seven birds – and nine hares and seven rabbits. Tom and Hugh counted the corpses, laid out in rows, and were complimented by Dan. A good morning, thanks to Master Tom and Master Hugh, who had beaten them gentlemen and Sir Robert.

Lady Hatton, Laura and Margaret welcomed the shooting party to lunch in the front parlour of Dan's cottage. This front room had been designed and furnished by Lady Hatton's father for no other purpose, and was never otherwise used. The lunch, served by Walter and Albert, was simple: hot Irish stew, apple tart and rice-pudding, washed down with beer and glasses of port for the grown-ups. The beaters got bread and cheese and a glass of beer in a nearby stooked cornfield.

Later that afternoon, towards tea-time, the shooting party returned to Stanford Hall. Laura, home before them, met Tom and Hugh at the back door and called them mysteriously upstairs. A letter had arrived for Tom, marked 'On His Majesty's Service'. She had it here for him.

They all waited anxiously while he read. He seemed to need time to take in what the letter said; then he looked up:

'I've been given a commission in the County regiment. I'm to report on the twenty-third.'

'Hurrah!' cried Hugh. 'The same day as I go to Dartmouth.'

'Lucky both of you,' Laura said.

'Laura, why not fall in with the idea of your going to the Pinewoods' convalescent home?' Hugh suggested. 'At least it would be something.'

'I don't want to,' Laura said slowly, 'but I may have to. As a first step.'

Meanwhile Tom had began to feel alarm at having opened his letter before his father was even aware of its arrival. Laura examined the envelope and said that they could stick it up again with the letter inside and put it back on the hall table. This they did.

So, after dinner that evening, Sir Robert cleared his throat and said, 'There has been a letter for you, Tom, which I opened.' All were silent as he produced it from his pocket. 'My good friend, Harold Pinewood, has secured you a commission in our County regiment, and you report on September the twenty-third. Here is your letter, boy.'

'Thank you, Papa,' Tom said, beaming. Laura and Hugh looked down at the table-cloth. Their mother had an air of sad pride: evidently she already knew of the contents of the letter. Everybody had known, in fact.

Sir Robert had more to say: 'Harold Pinewood and one or two other influential people have been putting pressure upon me. It has been a question of an extremely important post in the north – the coordination of munitions there. My family connexion with the coal and iron industries is a contributory factor.' He would not trouble himself to explain more to them, but added, 'In short, the appointment has been offered, and I have decided to take it.'

This was the first that Lady Hatton had been allowed to hear of such a plan. She was startled. 'But what about Stanford?'

'The agent will look after the estate, and I can come down occasionally to see to business affairs. But, as a family, we shall be living in the house in Yorkshire. It's much smaller, but that's no bad thing. We can run it comfortably on five servants. There is stabling for only three horses; but there again, we have lost our best horses to the army anyway.'

Laura was staring at her father, biting her lip as she did so. If she found no way out of this, she would be leaving Stanford only to go to that poky house which had belonged to Grandmama Hatton, with no park, no river, no country lanes to ride in.

She would not.

The permitted alternative was to go to the Pinewoods'. She knew that her father would positively encourage her in this, since he valued the Pinewood connexion so highly.

She chewed her lip, regardless of the inelegance, while she turned over in her mind the beginning of a plan, while the others talked – or rather, listened deferentially to Sir Robert.

After their four children had gone to bed, Sir Robert and Lady Hatton continued to talk of the future: he with jubilation; she with foreboding.

Sir Robert said: 'Harold Pinewood made a great point of its being such a waste not to use my brains in the present crisis. There are, after all, plenty of young men like his son and ours who can do the actual fighting.'

Lady Hatton replied only absently; she was asking herself, 'What is to become of Stanford?' and she was nerving herself desperately to fight for it.

15

SUDDENLY everything was changing at Stanford. Only those who lived on both sides of the baize doors knew how much. The children had been told of the plans that their father was making. They also knew, through Walter and Albert, of the fight which their mother was putting up not to leave Stanford; and they knew that she was losing the battle.

They knew that Walter did not intend to go with Sir Robert to Yorkshire. He would find a suitable post – plenty were always advertised – in the part of the country to which he had become accustomed. But he would be quite prepared to re-enter Sir Robert's service after the war, when the family returned to Stanford Hall. Thus, in the privacy of the butler's pantry, Walter sketched out to them his dignified speech of resignation.

Some time before it happened, they knew that James Pervis, the under-groom, was going to join up. They were agog to know their father's reception of the news, for he had planned to take James with him into Yorkshire. When James said he was giving notice, Sir Robert said loudly, 'You can't'; but it turned out that James could, because he did.

They knew that William Kemble himself had told Sir Robert that he might have to join up some day, and that Sir Robert had said it was more important that he and her Ladyship should be properly looked after in Yorkshire, because he, Sir Robert, had such important work there to do for his country. William had said, 'Yes, Sir Robert,' as respectfully as usual; but Mrs Kemble told the children that he said you couldn't get behind the Kitchener notices, 'Your Country Needs You'. Mrs Kemble said that Kemble was like those nunting gentlemen when they heard the horn and the cry of the hounds, he would be off and stop at nothing; it would scare her stiff to jump some of them five-barred gates, but not William; and it was the same with those Kitchener notices.

They knew that Albert had decided to go up to Yorkshire to see Elsie settled in nicely, and then join up. That would mean a row and a half, Walter predicted.

The children were the only ones to know what Laura really meant to do. Publicly she had agreed to work in the Pinewoods' new convalescent home for officers, and Alice was helping her to prepare to pack: she would need a good many clothes, including two evening dresses, for the social life there. She had chosen to leave for the Pinewoods' on the same day as Tom and Hugh were leaving Stanford: they in the early morning; she in the afternoon.

The night before this departure, Laura went to bed early. The two boys said good night to their mother and father and went up by the front stairs; then they slipped down again by the back stairs to see Walter. He was alone in the pantry, Albert having gone to bed.

'We've come to say good-bye,' said Hugh, 'as we may not have time to say it properly in the morning. We shall miss you, Walter; we always do.'

'I miss you,' Walter said, 'and I suppose that's really why I'm not staying on; but it wouldn't do to say that to Sir Robert, would it? Anyway, when you come back, I'll come back – if Sir Robert will have me.'

'When Stanford is mine, I'll get you back, anyway,' Tom said boldly.

'What parties we'll have then!' Hugh cried. 'We'll go fishing; and we'll have real cricket matches with the village team; and we'll have boating parties; oh! and all kinds of things!'

Walter smiled and said, 'I think it's time you young gentlemen went to bed.'

'Yes,' Tom said, 'but first I must say good-bye to Elsie. I promised I would.'

'I think you'll find she's gone up by now.'

Tom looked worried at that, so Hugh cut short his farewell to Walter, and they went along together to the servants' hall; but it was dark and empty, and so was the kitchen.

'Oh!' said Tom. 'And I promised.'

The two went up the back stairs together and to their rooms, saying good night as they parted. It was not long before they were both in bed, and Hugh was asleep.

Tom could not get to sleep because of the remembrance of his promise. He had a feeling that Elsie might still be waiting, and certainly he had seen a reflection of light up in the attic storey when he and Hugh had passed the foot of the staircase that led to it.

He got out of bed again and put on his dressing-gown. He was pretty sure that his mother and father had gone to bed; but if he were caught, he could say he was only going to the lavatory. He lit his candle and crept out and along the passage. All was silent and there were no lights – not even the dim reflection he thought he had seen earlier. He hesitated on the landing leading to the attics where Elsie and the other servants slept. It was, of course, too dangerous to climb those stairs; but as he waited, his courage grew, and he began.

He had nearly reached the top when to his horror he saw a white-robed figure, silent, still. For a moment he thought it really was a ghost; but then the figure whispered, 'You promised to say good-bye, Master Tom.'

'Come down,' Tom whispered back; and she followed him.

'Oh, you do look scared!' Elsie said.

'Yes,' Tom said. 'I'm afraid of someone waking. I'm – I suppose I'm terrified. The palms of my hands are sweating.' He had never before spoken frankly to anyone about the kind of fear that he sometimes felt, and that he so despised himself for feeling.

'There's nothing to be afraid of,' Elsie said. 'They're all fast asleep.'

'I didn't recognize you,' Tom said. 'I've never seen you with your hair down and in a flannel nightgown. It makes you look different.' He put the candle down on the landing table, and with both hands put Elsie's long hair behind her shoulders and then clasped her round the waist and gently kissed her: 'Good-bye, Elsie.'

She said, 'Oh, Master Tom! You know, I sometimes dream about you, and I suppose that's why I stay on here, and I'll go on staying with her Ladyship and Sir Robert in Yorkshire, so as I'll know how you get on fighting the war; and when you come back to Stanford, I hope I'll be here.'

A cold shiver had gone down Tom's spine when Elsie spoke of his father and mother. What would they say if they saw him now? He could not imagine what punishment they would think right for him; but certainly Elsie would get the sack.

'No one must ever know that I kissed you,' said Tom. 'No one. Ever.'

'No,' said Elsie. She could feel that his warmth had gone and he was frightened again. 'Don't be so afraid. We ain't done nothing wrong.'

'Good-bye, Elsie dear.' Then quickly, 'I think I heard something.'

Elsie started up the stairs as quietly as she had descended, and Tom seized the candle and blew it out. The alarm was false, however. He waited until he thought that Elsie must be safely back along the attic passage, then he groped his way to his own bedroom.

Inside, he dared to relax. He went over to the window, pulled up the blind and looked across the park. In the moonlight, the great elms cast great shadows. He could hear the flowing of the river, and the occasional quack of a duck; and then an owl. The view was beautiful, mysterious, and somehow very frightening. He pulled the blind sharply down again and went to bed.

Laura lay awake; she had not slept since she came to bed. She was absorbed in this strange new sensation: her last night at Stanford! She had been born here, lived here, had never spent a single night away from here; and tomorrow she was going.

She had planned everything coolly, carefully, and with no advice or help from anyone. The other three were the only ones she had told, in strictest secrecy, when her preparations were complete.

She had known without inquiry that her parents would never, in the ordinary course of events, allow her to train as a proper nurse in a proper hospital. Rather than that, they would have carried her off to Yorkshire with them. So she had agreed to join with the other daughters of local gentry helping in the Pinewoods' convalescent home. She would stay there until her parents had gone north. Then she would remove herself and her luggage, which she was deliberately keeping to one small trunk, in spite of Alice's distracted protests: she would escape to the Honeford hospital. She had already written to the matron there, offering herself. There was no doubt that she would be accepted.

The only real risk, of course, lay in her parents. But she had calculated that, far away in Yorkshire, they would be more inclined to accept the accomplished fact of what she had done, and be equally disinclined to stir up a local scandal by trying to force her to leave the Honeford hospital. After all, to train as a nurse was patriotic. And, after all, she was really grown up. Tomorrow she would begin to prove that.

A distant clock struck twelve. Today she would prove herself. Laura closed her eyes and went to sleep.

The next morning she dissuaded Margaret from going

down to the courtyard to say good-bye to Tom and Hugh: 'You don't want Papa to see you crying, do you?'

So the sisters made their farewells in the schoolroom. Then, from the nursery window, they watched the parting between parents and sons. Lady Hatton cried a little; Sir Robert led her back indoors.

'I don't intend there to be anyone down there saying good-bye to me this afternoon,' Laura said.

She was as good as her word. When the time came, she told Margaret, 'I'll go down by the back stairs. Wait a little, and then go and tell Mama and Papa that I've gone.'

'But Mama will be so upset.'

'No, she won't. Tell her that I'll certainly write to her when they've settled in Yorkshire.'

At the door of their bedroom, where they had been talking, Laura paused. She turned and looked steadily, wonderingly, round the room; then she came back to kiss Margaret again, and this time she said, 'Meg, you mustn't be too sad without us all'; and was gone.

It was not exactly sadness that Margaret felt, after the first pangs of parting from them all; only strangeness – a great and terrifying strangeness. For the rest of that afternoon she wandered aimlessly about the gardens, and all the time she felt as if she were playing Wolf by herself, with no safe home to run to.

It seemed more sociable later, when Papa and Mama had left to motor up to Yorkshire. (As the car turned out through the gates Margaret had seen to her surprise that her mother was crying as if her heart would break.) Albert bolted and locked the front door behind them, and Walter said, 'Well, that's that. Come on, Miss Margaret, let's all go and ask Elsie for a cup of tea. We can put our feet up now.' Walter seized one hand and Albert the other, and they swung her along. She laughed with delight.

When they reached the servants' hall, Elsie was there, with Alice and the between-maid, and the little kitchen-maid, and Elsie said comfortably: 'Come on, Miss Margaret, sit down here. I've brewed us all a cup of tea, and her Ladyship said we might as well finish up the cakes.'

After tea Walter wanted to buy some tobacco in the village, and took Margaret with him. She held his hand all the way, and he gave her twopence to spend on chocolate. Then he saw her back into the park, saying, 'This is my great chance for a drink and a chat in the pub, you know.' Sir Robert disapproved of his staff visiting public-houses.

Margaret ran most of the way back across the park, because she was afraid of its getting dark and because she wanted to show Elsie her chocolate. But when she reached the kitchen, Elsie was out; so she went up to the schoolroom. All was quiet; there was nothing to do, nobody to talk to. She watched out of the window until outside grew dark. Then she turned up the lamp, and waited, with the door open, for her supper. As she sat, the schoolroom seemed to get larger and the passage outside wider and longer, like a dark street in a town. Then the between-maid came with her supper of soup and a cake. 'And Alice says, Go to bed when you have finished, and she will be up later.'

Margaret tried to persuade the maid to stay a while, but the servants' hall supper had to be got, and Elsie was still out. Margaret made her promise to ask Elsie to come up when she returned.

Alone again, Margaret ate her supper, then went along the passage to the bedroom, undressed and got into bed. Her candle was flickering and making odd shadows; and she did not like the look of Laura's bed under its dustsheets. It seemed a long time before Alice came and tucked her up and said, 'You must get to sleep now. You've a long journey tomorrow.'

'Isn't Elsie back yet?'

'Not yet. She will be soon; and then we'll all be going to bed. We've had a long day, and I've a lot to do tomorrow after you go.' Alice was staying on at Stanford as caretaker, on the understanding that Dan Power would be there every night to ward off burglars. 'Now blow out your candle, Miss Margaret.'

'Will you leave the door open?'

'But there's no light in the passage. In fact, I'd better shut it in case you sleep-walk.' Then, noticing the expression on Margaret's face, Alice added, 'There's nothing to be afraid of. Mr Mark will be downstairs as usual, and the rest of us are all up in the attics if you want anything.'

Alice said good night and shut the door. Margaret wanted to call her back, on any pretence; but Alice was not the kind you could persuade against her will. If only Elsie had come; but she had not.

Last night there had been Laura in the same room, and Tom and Hugh along the passage. Why had everyone forsaken her?

She lay for what seemed hours listening to her own heartbeats, afraid of her own breathing. Her candle had been left burning, but would not last all night. At last she summoned courage to get out of bed, go to the door and open it. The passage was dark and she could see no light from the back stairs. She was afraid to go further, and went back to bed. She began calling, 'Elsie – Elsie –Elsie!' No one heard; no one came; no one would ever come. She was sobbing now as she called. Then quite suddenly there were quick footsteps and Elsie's voice: 'Whatever is the matter?'

'Oh, Elsie, I thought you would never come!'

'Miss, miss! You shouldn't work yourself up into such a state. I would have come earlier, but we don't often get a night off; and when I come in, Alice told me you would be asleep, and Mr Mark and Albert and me were just having a last cup of tea down in the pantry.'

'Don't leave me now, Elsie.'

'That I won't, miss. Not till you're asleep, leastways. But I shall have to get to bed myself. I've to be up early, and we have this long railway journey to Yorkshire.'

'Read me a story.'

'I can't read books very well,' said Elsie, 'but let's go into the schoolroom and see what we can find.'

In the schoolroom Elsie held her candle up to whatever she thought might amuse and soothe Margaret. 'Oh, look! I love that photo of Master Tom when he was little – and this one of you all, years ago, only you all look so miserable with that German governess keeping you in order.'

'I wish we were all together now,' Margaret said still tearfully.

Elsie moved on and lifted the lid of a polished mahogany box. 'Aren't these Master Hugh's birds' eggs?'

'Yes, and that very big one is the heron's egg. It's rather a rarity, Hugh says.'

'And here's your doll's house. I longed and longed to play with it myself when I first came here.'

'I've never played with it much, because Laura didn't care for it, and nor did the boys, of course.'

'Let's play now,' said Elsie. Together they knelt on the floor and opened the front of the little house. 'Oh, isn't it sweet! The bedroom with the four-poster bed in it and all; and the dining-room with the chairs and table, with the lady and gentleman sitting down to dinner with their plates and knives and spoons and forks, but nothing to eat.'

'I like the kitchen best,' Margaret said, growing interested. 'I like the range with all those little saucepans and the cook standing beside them. She makes me think of you, Elsie.'

'Oh, dear, miss! The cook looks very old with that grey hair – more like Alice; I hope I've another fifty years before I look like that. But, anyway, let's tidy up this room with the dollies in it – two little boys and a little girl. I think this must be their nursery or schoolroom, don't you?'

Together they removed the dolls and furniture, shook the tiny carpet and relaid it, dusted, cleaned. For half an hour they were absorbed and happy in their work. When at last they shut the front of the house again, Elsie held her candle close to a window and said, 'Look in, Miss Margaret. You can see how comfortable they all look now. Those children want to go to sleep, as you do now.'

'Good night, Tom, Hugh, and Laura,' Margaret said. 'They look a little like them, don't they?'

'Now come, miss,' said Elsie, and led Margaret gently back to her bedroom and to bed.

But suddenly, in bed, Margaret said, 'I can't – I *can't* sleep here alone. Sleep here with me, Elsie, in Laura's bed.'

'Oh, I daren't do that!' Elsie said. 'Whatever would Alice say, or her Ladyship, to my sleeping down here!' But even as she spoke, Elsie realized that in fact she could sleep here: sleep in Miss Laura's bed and along the passage from Master Tom's own room. 'All right, miss, I'll make up the bed.' In a few moments it was done, and Margaret contentedly watched Elsie pull off her cotton dress and take off her shoes and black stockings. In her woollen combinations she went over to kiss Margaret good night.

'Would you like a nightgown?' Margaret asked. 'There's probably one of Laura's in the drawer.'

'No, dear,' said Elsie. 'This was always good enough for us at home.' She blew out their candles and got into bed; in only a few moments she could hear from Margaret's breathing that she was asleep.

Elsie lay awake a little longer, thinking. Suppose her mother could see her in this bed, in this room now! She often wondered what her mother and father would say if they saw the beds and the carpets and the plate – and above all the food that came into the house. The food! Dan Power carried in half a dozen rabbits three or four times a week. Pheasants and partridges in season; she had never sat down to one, but she had tasted both. Then Mr Phillips – oh! the fruit and vegetables he brought to the house, but half the brussels sprouts were chucked away because they tired of them on the other side of the baize door. No wonder the odd man went through the refuse bin before emptying it. His wife made soup from the mutton bones and other good scraps. Elsie could just imagine how her mother would have liked to get at that bin . . .

Beds and carpets and rabbits and pheasants and brussels sprouts and the faces of the odd man and of her mother and of Master Tom when he kissed her – all slowly circled and blended inside Elsie's drowsy head; and at last she was asleep too.

The next morning they went off with Albert; and then Walter went; and then the shutters of Stanford Hall were closed and barred, the blinds drawn; no lights could be seen after dark; no feet heard regularly up and down the back and front stairs. The bells in the kitchen passage were silent, and only one chimney showed any smoke.

In the servants' hall Alice sat listening to the ticking of the clock, and waiting for Dan. And when she had gone to bed, Dan lay on a mattress in the great hall, with Jet on one side and his gun on the other, waiting for burglars and for the day when Master Tom and Master Hugh would return to shoot partridges and pheasants and them vermin.

EPILOGUE

No children live at Stanford Hall now.

No one lives here except the old caretaker and his wife. In summer he shows coachloads of sightseers round the state rooms of the house, pointing out its treasures, answering questions. Always among sightseers there is someone who asks, 'And do the family still live here?'

No, the caretaker answers. The owner, elderly, unmarried, lives abroad.

One day, after a tour of the house is finished, a visitor has other questions to ask: 'I knew the elder son, Tom, was killed in the First World War: it was in all the papers at the time, of course, because of his being awarded the V.C. afterwards. But I heard no more of the family. Why doesn't Hugh Hatton live here now?'

'He was killed in the war, too, sir.'

'Killed in the war! But he was only a child!'

'Sixteen. A midshipman at sixteen. Killed in action at sea.'

'Poor Hugh! And I was still a schoolboy . . .'

The caretaker looks curiously at the stranger, wondering, sizing him up: a man getting on a bit in years; well dressed; well educated – oh! you can tell that; a man with a position in the world . . . 'You were a friend of the family, sir?'

'Only of the children – of Hugh, really.'

'I was footman here, sir. Albert Barker is the name.' He pauses expectantly, but the stranger does not respond. So Albert goes on: 'The war was very hard on the family, sir. Miss Laura – did you know she became a nurse?'

'No. I can imagine she made a first-class one.'

'Died of some hospital fever just before the Armistice. So you see, sir, it was Miss Margaret that inherited – she that least wanted it. She nearly broke her heart when the others died. Sir Robert and his lady they were set on her marrying to have an heir for Stanford, but she never would. Awful rows there used to be – but that's in the past, sir. Sir Robert and her Ladyship died many years ago. Miss Margaret's tried several times since then to live here on her own, but it makes her too unhappy. The last time, she told my wife she wouldn't come again because of the others.'

'The others?'

'The other three children – but not their ghosts – nothing like that. No, she says to my wife – she's fond of my wife, sir, from the old days – she says it's that the house remembers.'

'*The house remembers* . . .' The visitor repeats the words, staring at the house-front before him, the empty windows; he goes on staring.

'You'll miss your coach, sir. Everyone else is in.'

'I'm not going by coach. If there is no objection, I am walking across the park to Stanford village. Someone there – one of my family . . .'

'Yes, sir?'

'My sister lies buried in the churchyard. She died as a child: Evie Tomlin.'

So the visitor begins his solitary walk across the park: in the late afternoon sunshine the elms cast long shadows; a duck quacks from the direction of the river; he listens for the sound of the water, but his hearing is not as good as when he was a boy.

The caretaker has turned back into Stanford Hall. All the visitors are gone now, and he begins to shutter and bolt and lock up. His wife usually helps him in this and now he begins to call her.

'Elsie – Elsie – Elsie!'

In the empty house the echo of the name prolongs itself, fainter and fainter, but clear – clear, like a memory of past lives.